When
Harry met
Meghan

When Harry met Meghan

The untold story of everything that probably didn't happen

CAROL STRATHCONA

THE CLOISTER HOUSE PRESS

First published in the United Kingdom in 2021 by
The Cloister House Press

ISBN 978-1-913460-24-2

The events in this collection of short stories are purely fictional. If anything should come close to reality, this is the result of mere coincidence.

The stories told here are in some parts cynical, probably even a bit grotesque. Being a comedy, though, the book will hopefully put a smile on the reader's face.

Contents

The Blind Date

The rain was dripping monotonously onto the roof of the taxi. The sound of splashing water spilled out from the tyres of passing cars, intermingling with the familiar sound of the engine slowing down in front of yet another traffic light.

Today was a day like many other days, busy and giving her the feeling of always being a little too short of time, and yet everything looked different. Even smelled and felt different. The colours seemed more intense, the sounds clearer and the taste in the air promising. Since she had first got up, her only thoughts had been circling around one topic. It was the day of the blind date.

Meghan was nervous. Should she really trust her friend and go on this blind date? She was staying in London for a few days, a short break during a business trip. Later in the week she would have to meet another agent for a new movie project. How dull: another casting.

She was totally on her own here in this vibrant European city, but that was more than OK. Back in America, there was always someone around her. Being on her own, able to make the decision of what to do and where and when to eat, was refreshing. She loved her temporary freedom.

Casting and acting were so strenuous. They could also be fun, but most of the time she'd be told what to do, and that wasn't really compatible with Meghan's personality.

She was a free spirit, eager to take her own decisions, as she had always done in her life. She was her one and only master, and she liked the idea of being independent and free.

She managed to bring her straying thoughts back to what was coming up shortly: this blind date.

Well ... she'd rather not think about it too much. And within a split second her mind was more than willing to be back at the casting.

But no, she forced herself to bring her mind to this awkward thing. *Oh, the blind date ...*

The only thing she knew so far was that his name was Harry and that he was supposedly rather famous. Of course, she had caught herself wondering several times who that guy might be. A few Harrys came to her mind: Harry Styles, Harry Belafonte, Harry Potter ...

While her thoughts were straying, she paid the taxi driver and suddenly realised that she had given him too much as a tip. But it was already too late. When she turned around and waved her hand, it was just in time to catch the sight of the taxi swinging sharply round the next corner. Her absent mind had associated the payment with her last visit to Mexico and the amount she had paid for a taxi ride in pesos. And now she had just given the taxi driver the same amount, but in pounds, which was far too much. Well, at least it had served its purpose, she tried to tell herself.

And here she was: the location of her blind date.

The unease came back and her knees weakened.

As she took the stairs to the upper floor of the elegant hotel, she felt somewhat strange. For the first time in her life, she was up to something she had not decided on herself. But then why? She had met plenty of men who had attempted to convince her into a date, and she always refused. But somehow her very good friend had been able to persuade her into this strange venture.

She preferred not to think of how disastrously this could end. Still, it was a blind date, and that was the risk. And, who knows, perhaps her counterpart would feel the same. The thought helped to calm her down a bit.

As she walked over the thin carpet, the noise of old wooden floor underneath made her feel more at ease. It sounded so familiar and comforting to her, although she had never lived in such an old house before. The creaking made her think of an elderly, friendly woman, and instantly she was back to her full strength. She knew that a woman's power was infinite.

Yes, I am going to manage this! Have I ever not managed anything in my life? Let's do it.

She was still tense, though: almost nervy. Under her transparent silk blouse, of which she had deliberately opened one or two buttons too many, she could feel her heart hammer. But the way she was dressed made her feel sexy. And independent. And invincible. Oddly enough, she welcomed her rapid heartbeat; it evoked the feeling of a forthcoming adventure.

She carried on down the corridor and suddenly stopped. This had to be the right room, as there was only one further door at the far back, and she could tell from where she was standing that the further door could only be the bathroom. At the reception desk they had told her to take the large door on the right, which would lead into the old library. Presumably quite a big room, comparing the size of the wall with the number of doors. In fact, the

3

room behind the door had to take up almost the entire length of the house.

*

Harry was looking out of the window. The sight was a bit uninspiring with the rain washing away the colours of today's moments, even washing away the movements of people rushing by on the concrete underneath. Everybody tried to escape the windy and miserable weather.

But Harry was in a perfectly good mood. A smile rushed over his lips as he anticipated the upcoming experience. He liked adventure and unpredictable things. In fact, since childhood he had always been prepared for the worst. When the time for a trained-for situation finally arrived, he had found that things often turned out better than anticipated.

He didn't mind being at the mercy of a situation he was not able to control. Actually, during most of his life, he had been in such situations. As a royal, one had to deal with that. One was always told what to do. Well, it did depend on whether one stuck to what one was told or decided to bend the rules a little bit.

Harry smiled again. Of course, he did not always stick to what was expected of him. Hence, in many a situation he had been forced into, he had managed to find the liberty to do what he wanted and not necessarily what he had been told to do.

Therefore, nothing could cause any fear in him. On the contrary, he liked this game and he approached such situations playfully, more often than not provoking as opposed to preventing them. He thrilled on being thrown into an uncontrollable situation, not least because he was always able to steer himself out in a way he wanted. This gave him security and independence. And he liked the kick.

His shining blue eyes roved the room. Most of the library was made of dark wooden panels, which gave the atmosphere a bit of a mysterious touch and at the same time made it cosy. Maybe it wouldn't be too bad to have some dim light for this first encounter; it could help to overcome a few outer insecurities.

Knowing that most women were hopeless romantics, Harry made a wonderful crackling fire in the highly decorated fireplace. Looking at the flames made him feel relaxed, his eyes getting warm and watery. He was caught up in lovely childhood memories of when he would sit in front of their fireplace at Kensington Palace, embraced by his unforgettable and adorable mother.

He looked at his watch and it was time! He took a seat on the purple velvet vintage chair which was standing next to him. He was dressed in casual jeans and open shirt, looking relaxed. A smart jacket gave him the look of being dressed for a date. A date. What a lovely invention. Harry could date every day. 'Life changes quickly and chances are new,' he sang quietly to himself.

At that moment, he heard a shy knock on the door and thought, *Well, the staff have finally brought the drinks I ordered.* He didn't turn around; he just muttered a grumpy 'Come in' through a mouth fenced with a jungle of hair.

He didn't know it was his date who had knocked on the door and who opened it with a bold, smooth movement.

*

As she stepped into the room, Meghan was struck with shock. The only thing she was able to make out in the dim light was a shape from behind. Against the light, it rather looked like a toilet brush turned upside-down. What on earth was this man wearing on his head?

He didn't seem to have noticed her, as he neither spoke nor turned around. She backed out of the room as quickly as she could. In the corridor she gasped for air. Gee, that surely had to be the wrong door!

She hurried down the stairs back to reception, almost falling down the steps in her body-tight skirt, taking two steps at once.

*

Well, that was fast, Harry thought. He turned around but could not spot where they had placed the drinks. He shook his head, getting impatient. Another look at the watch gave him a hot shot through the veins. Time was already up, his blind date about to come in any moment, but there were still no drinks here. He took the receiver of the phone that was standing on one of the side tables and nervously dialled reception.

*

Meghan had asked for directions to the right room and hadn't liked the answer. She was hesitantly walking back up the steps to the upper floor, a bit shaky on her skyscraper-like high heels, heading back to the room she had just ran away from. Everything was getting out of hand and she was not the master of the situation. Should she turn around and take the first taxi back to her hotel? For a moment the thought was very tempting.

and most natural way, displaying her freshly bleached teeth.

Harry swallowed once more and said, 'Hi, I'm Harry.'

His beard was trembling as he muttered the words. He was beguiled by her enchanting smile and was ready to drown in that feeling forever.

AND SO IT ALL BEGAN ...

The Dogs

Harry had learnt from friends that pets play an essential role in a fresh relationship. In fact, the relationship can live or die on whether they accept the new partner of their master.

Harry had also learnt from his grandmother, the Queen, how important animals could be. She loved her corgis above all and he knew, having been barked at for over thirty years, how distracting this could be when visiting her. Of course, one was never allowed to say anything against her darlings!

Meghan, however, came, saw and conquered. Whenever she met dogs on the street, they loved her from the beginning. No barking, no growling, only wagging tails. Harry was certain that the Queen would be delighted when her dogs immediately came to love Meghan, and that his grandmother would instantaneously love Meghan in turn.

And then the horses! How fond his grandma was of these beautiful and sensitive creatures. Luckily, Harry and his brother William happened to be excellent riders and polo players, much to the amusement of the Queen.

Meghan also called two dogs her own, and this made Harry frown. Even more so because they were male. A male would always see another male as a potential rival, even a dog and a human being. This thought made Harry nervous and caused him a few sleepless nights.

not be the first time Harry had done something that did not make any sense at all.

*

Harry was back in a cheerful mood, carrying some sausages in his luggage, whistling the melody of today's favourite pop song again.

He felt very well prepared for the trip to Canada. The prospect of seeing Meghan was starting to stir up a very nervous but still quite pleasant feeling in his stomach area. He was full of anticipation, knowing that nothing could prevent him from winning over those dogs with unparalleled speed and skill.

He smiled and bobbed his head while speeding up to the gate, mentally rehearsing all the tricks he had to master to get to the goal. As always, nothing was free in life, except for the best things like happiness and love, both of which he currently had lots of. He almost stumbled in his eagerness as he galloped through the open door of the aircraft. He happily took his seat far in the back of the plane and pulled his cap a bit lower over his face so that nobody was able to recognise him, and he started to drift away, dreaming of Meghan's beautiful smile as she introduced him to Bogart and Guy.

A very loud barking sound made Harry jump in his seat. Completely disoriented, he looked to his side and found a carry-on basket from which a small and aggressive dog bared its teeth, growling at him.

Horrified, he fled to the toilet, trying to recover his poise. Why the hell was he always in the spotlight of a dog's attention?

Harry's face was pale when he returned to his seat,

trying hard to fight his stirring feelings. The dog's owner must have taken the seat next to him while he had been dozing, not noticing the build-up of this emergency situation. Now he was trapped here. The plane was fully booked, and it would be hopeless to ask the flight attendants to change his seat.

He unwillingly took his seat again, from which he would have to endure the unfriendly dog for all of the many hours this long-haul flight was going to take.

Harry felt like he had been tortured by the time he disembarked, not having been able to close his eyes again en route after the first dog confrontation. He was completely out of his comfort zone by now, and he would be meeting Meghan in a few minutes.

After a speedy bathroom visit, he knew that unfortunately nothing would put him back at ease and help improve his poor outer appearance, which mirrored his inner feelings. Still, he would somehow manage to lift himself out of this miserable situation. Harry put his shoulders back in one smooth movement, put on his charming smile, grabbed his luggage and strode towards the welcome hall for international arrivals.

*

Harry was shivering. He had to grab the first opportunity to make friends with the dogs. This was *the* crucial moment to win their hearts.

Kneeling on the bright kitchen floor, he fumbled in his pocket, nervously trying to find the pack of sausages he was hiding there. Unsuccessful, he pulled back his hand and tried the other pocket. But his hand still found no relief, his heartbeat picking up. The bloody bangers weren't in either of his pockets! Where the hell had he put them?

The dogs had noticed with anticipation that Harry was planning to feed them something. They wagged their tails, getting closer, their noses wet and their mouths watering.

Harry was getting more and more irritated. He tried to clear his thoughts and think. The jet lag didn't help with his misery. In his mind he went back to the bathroom at the airport where he had had his last chance to prepare secretly for this match point. Beads of perspiration started to build on his forehead.

The dogs were getting impatient, thinking Harry was deliberately teasing them, which they didn't like at all.

Harry's mind was working at the speed of light, but still he was not able to recall where he had put those idiotic sausages in his hurry. The only things he had found in his pockets were a packet of tissues and a melted chocolate bar. In the rush at the airport he must have grabbed the wrong things from his luggage.

One of the dogs started to bark. At first playfully, then louder and more demanding, thinking Harry was a cruel man, teasing him without feeding him afterwards.

Harry started to whistle, trying to distract himself and the dogs, trying to convey that nothing was wrong at all.

This made the dogs even angrier. What was this human being thinking? They were used to getting attention after being offered food, and this man's behaviour was not fair!

The second dog joined the barking and they both got louder and louder, Harry growing smaller and smaller at the same time.

Why was everything so difficult with him and dogs? He just didn't understand. He was so willing to give them pleasure, and the only thing he got in return was aggressive behaviour.

Their gentle yaps had turned into a menacing roar.

At this point, the kitchen door was flung open and a very upset Meghan sped into the room. 'Harry, what's going on? What are you doing to my doggies?'

Harry, very, very embarrassed, stammered, 'Oh, just playing funcle: you know, fun uncle, like with George.'

'This isn't funny, Harry; you have to treat my dogs like they're adults. I told you, they are not stupid creatures.'

As if they wanted to make the already tragic moment even more dramatic, the dogs ran to Meghan like a baby to Mummy, looking for shelter at her knees, sending dark glances to Harry. Harry was devastated, but he swore to give it another try.

*

Harry was royal enough not to allow himself to be daunted by this unlucky experience. After all, he was of noble birth and capable of dealing with almost every seemingly hopeless situation.

He regained courage, and on another occasion – Meghan was out shopping for some food – he made another attempt, all well prepared and thinking positively, having forgotten his bad start.

Kneeling down on the marble tiles, he grabbed the (this time carefully stored) pack of sausages and called Bogart and Guy. As they ran towards him, he suddenly started to feel a cramp creeping up his body, an anxiety likely to seize him. He managed to stay calm, opened the packet and took out a sausage.

In this very moment, Meghan's voice was heard in the

corridor, singing, 'Oh, my dear dearies, where are the three of you? Did you hide? Where are all my darlings?'

In a movement close to a panic attack, Harry shoved the uncooked sausage into his own mouth, trying not to show Meghan what he had been up to. He needed a Meghan accusing him of trying to corrupt her animals like a bullet through his head.

In only a few bites, the sausage was down his throat, the only sign it had ever been there his short, disgusted swallow as Meghan entered. Bogart and Guy were complaining in stereo.

'Oh, Harry, darling, I came back as some friends just called and invited us for dinner, so no shopping needed today,' she purred, before she looked at her dogs and her face fell in complete disbelief. She raised her voice. 'Harry, what did I tell you? Do not hurt my darlings. I don't like how you treat them!'

With a disapproving look at Harry, she caressed Bogart and Guy, who were whimpering in a heartbreaking manner. This cruel man had been eating a delicious sausage in front of them, tormenting them again.

What made matters worse was that Harry started to feel very sick as they prepared to go out. He felt the raw sausage lying heavily in his stomach, with his digestive system struggling to deal with this unusual food, but tried not to let Meghan suspect the tiniest thing. He had been able to sense her tension since this afternoon's Doggygate.

Before they met Meghan's friends, she was going to take Harry for a drink at a famous bar. Meghan was eager to show Harry the best locations in town and to let him be part of her life. She was chatting and giggling non-stop,

21

sharing her insider knowledge. This consumed an amount of time that was not to be underestimated.

While Meghan elegantly sipped her drink, Harry started to feel more and more uneasy, his stomach rebelling at the smell of food every time someone was served something to eat. He tried to fight it, his beard starting to tremble, small drops of perspiration appearing between the rust-coloured hairs of it.

'Darling, is something wrong?' Meghan asked, worried.

'No, sweetheart, all is well. It's probably the jet lag. I feel like I have a hole in my stomach. Or perhaps it's just because I am so nervous around you.'

Meghan seductively opened her wet lips and slowly shoved a baked cheese bar into her mouth. 'Oh, honey, you make me feel hot. Maybe we'll cancel the invitation and head out for a quick fix. We could have a hot dog to take away around the corner, then we can go home and make ourselves comfy. What do you think?'

Hearing the phrase *hot dog* was the end; it was too much for poor Harry. Hardly able to contain himself, he hurried to the bathroom, bending down over the lavatory in the last second and reverse-swallowing the dog sausage in a huge explosion of pain.

Coming back paler than the white tiles on the floor, he very much agreed to leave this institution, but with bed as the immediate destination, leaving Meghan to worry endlessly about what was going wrong.

*

Harry was in utter distress. Since he had eaten the sausage himself, the dogs distrusted him in every respect and there was no way of trying to feed them any more. Guy and Bogart had started to eye Harry suspiciously; every movement he made was under their scrutiny. Even when he slept, they kept tracking each breath he took. Of course, this didn't help Harry feel better; no, it tortured him, knowing that Meghan might have increasing doubts about him as a partner.

He still needed to get them onto his side, knowing that Meghan disliked how his relationship with the dogs had evolved so far. This put him under even more pressure. In a last desperate attempt, he decided to call England.

Harry dialled the number of Anmer Hall, his hands shaking wildly.

'Oh, hello, Kate, how are you? Well, everything is just fantastic here; Meghan and I enjoy every moment together, no stress at all. Yeah, we are already like a family, she and her two dogs and me. Oh, by the way, the dogs are starting to get bored with me feeding them all the time, you know. Do you know how to catch their attention again? I mean, I want to keep them amused. And they are so fond of the sausages you recommended!'

'Oh, Harry, that's fantastic news. I am so glad that you and Meghan and the dogs are having a wonderful time. Well, to improve your relationship with the doggies, you could try to pretend to be one of them.'

Harry frowned, the painful memory of reverse-swallowing the unpleasant sausage coming back to his tormented mind. 'Be one of them ...?'

Silence.

'I mean, I already tried, and it was not good.' In his mind he added a silent, agonised yell.

'What do you mean?' Kate asked. 'Did you really go down on all fours and try to be part of their group? Every newcomer has to be accepted by the pack; that's nature. Go and try again!'

Harry didn't know how to thank Kate for her wise advice. Immediately, he gained strength and hope, knowing that his time would finally come.

*

The day came when Harry was in the perfect mood, able to prove what he had learnt about dogs in his young life. Meghan was out again, and so he started to crawl on all fours, panting in different pitches, trying to copy the behaviour he had studied from the two dogs so far. He had managed to tie the kitchen brush to the back of his belt, trying to simulate a tail. He whirled his back to the right and the left in very quick movements, saliva dripping from his mouth, making begging noises.

Bogart and Guy were offended. Now, this cruel human being had even started to make fun of them, trying to make them feel inferior by mocking their behaviour. This was too much to bear; this was the very end! Bogart and Guy escaped from the kitchen immediately, rushed to the balcony and alarmed the whole neighbourhood with their shouting.

When Meghan came back, her apartment door was wide open. Accelerating her steps, she found a devastated Harry trying to calm down her barking dogs, while a neighbour, being a very experienced dog owner herself, tried to keep the dogs from attacking Harry.

'Haaaa-rriiiiiiii, what are you doing to my darlings? I told you to respect them!'

Meghan's expression failed to show any sign of pity for the whining Harry as she welcomed her dogs, which were standing up and wagging their tails to greet her.

Even in the darkest hour, a small light often flickers. Harry still saw some light at the end of the tunnel, and he swore by the Crown that he would not give up. One day, he would have the chance to prove his dog skills! Not today, maybe not tomorrow, but one day in the future. A very shaky hope was stirring, growing slowly but steadily: his dog day was sure to come.

Wellygate

For the first time, Meghan was visiting Harry at Kensington Palace. Harry was eager to introduce his love to his place.

After taking Meghan on a tour of their new home, Nottingham Cottage – which had actually taken only two minutes as it was so tiny – Harry felt a sense of release. Meghan seemed to like it, although it was not a palace. Harry liked the simple things and he always felt comfortable in this cosy place.

The burning love between Harry and Meghan was fresh and new, both still a bit shy and embarrassed here at the beginning of their relationship. They had just cosily installed themselves on the sofa when Harry received a phone call. It seemed to take a long time.

After a while, Meghan decided to sneak upstairs to use the bathroom. As the house provided precisely one bathroom with one toilet, sink and shower, it was easy for her to find it again.

With a little trepidation, she lifted the seat and discovered to her relief that everything looked nice and clean. Sitting on the toilet, she let her eyes rove around and discovered some strange slimy tracks over the window. Looking closer, she detected that a few of them even happened to cross the walls of the bathroom – on the inside. Meghan started to wonder.

She allowed herself time and, when she pulled the long chain of the vintage toilet, a strong flush made any other sound inaudible. Meghan washed her hands in the lovely sink with two separate taps – one for hot, one for cold water – which made her wonder why this separation existed. Nevertheless, she thoroughly enjoyed this atmosphere of bygone times.

A sudden knock on the door interrupted her daydreaming, Harry asking with emphasis whether he was allowed to enter. Meghan frowned; was she doing anything wrong?

She opened the door and looked innocently at a seemingly upset Harry.

'Did you now just use this toilet?' he asked her impatiently.

'Well, yes, I thought, well, er, I had to use it. Why?'

'OK, fair point, but I'm afraid you missed one essential thing!'

'Essential thing?'

'Yeah, I'll show you ...'

Harry went over to the tiny cupboard, opened the door, browsed through it for a few seconds and pulled out some kind of plastic gadget. What, for heaven's sake, was this 'thing', Meghan wondered.

'You have to learn one thing: before using *any* toilet, even this one, you have to use *this*,' Harry explained, emanating the air of an experienced, wise professor, pointing with his long forefinger at the 'thing'.

Meghan frowned.

With a swift movement he opened the thing's cover and produced some type of ring made of plastic or rubber. He pointed to one spot which was clearly marked in red, pulled out a small tube and opened its flip top. He took a deep breath and with a whistling sound blew a lungful of air into the thing, which after a couple of repetitions unfolded into an inflatable toilet seat.

At first Meghan was surprised and laughed, then she started to get suspicious. Was Harry kidding her?

'Before sitting down, you always use this inflatable toilet seat and put it over mine. It is essential for your health and safety, and there is no exception at all!! From now on you will always carry one with you when you go out, and you can keep a fully inflated one for use at home!' Harry whirled around, fumbled again in the cupboard and proudly produced another folded package with a second toilet seat. 'You will have your own carved wooden one in due course and a separate WC installed for your private use only. Until then, you must use this inflatable one, even at home.'

'Harry, are you serious? I mean ...' It was hard not to giggle.

Harry made it very clear that he was utterly serious and she should stick to this rule.

Meghan's frown deepened.

'What is it, Meghan? Do you think you can manage this on your own, or should we practise? We can do it right now,' Harry suggested.

'Oh, no, Harry, I think you made yourself quite clear. I guess I can manage,' Meghan answered, staring in embarrassed disbelief at the awkward thing in her hands.

As the evening went by, Meghan's jet lag started to creep up on her and she decided to retire, as far as that was possible in this tiny place.

'Why don't you stay here on the couch while I prepare

for bed?' she whispered to Harry. 'I have a little surprise for you ...' She smiled at him with great promise.

Harry didn't hesitate to agree. Meghan went up the stairs, and he waited ...

And waited ...

A rustling noise came from upstairs, and Harry drifted away into his wildest fantasies of romantic underwear.

More noise could be heard from upstairs, like a jump into bed and the bedsheets shifting. Harry was hardly able to contain himself any more, feeling his body tightening in anticipation.

Finally, the releasing command came from upstairs, inviting him to bed. Harry almost flew up the stairs, taking three steps at once.

When he entered the bedroom, it was all dark as Meghan had shut the blinds. Just vaguely, he was able to make out that she was lying under the sheets.

Harry approached, a big smile on his bright face. He couldn't wait to touch her beautiful skin and body. He had been longing for this moment constantly since he had last seen her.

Getting rid of his shoes, trousers and socks, leaving only his underpants and a T-shirt, Harry started to sneak into the bed from the bottom, lifting up the cover only slightly and crawling in underneath. He crawled up a bit further until he could feel parts of her, which attracted every single fibre of his body; he was hardly able to control it any longer.

'Oh, Meghan, I love your skin. It is so soft; this is such a wonderful feeling ...' His hands travelled from her thighs down to her lower legs.

Meghan murmured something indistinct from underneath the cover. Harry didn't mind; body language was completely sufficient at this time, his hand travelling down further and further.

Harry moved up in bed, his hands now moving towards her breasts while he caressed her legs with his feet. The soft touch of her lower legs almost made him jump. He was thrilled and electrified.

'Oh, Meghan, did you just shave your legs for me?'

Again, it was hard to make out her reply.

Harry decided to turn around and crawl back to those delightful legs to appreciate more of her silk-like skin. It was then that an unforeseen incident almost put a stop to the whole venture. Totally absorbed in the experience, he lost more and more control of his body, until a loud explosive sound from the outlet of his own digestion made him jump like only a sudden gunshot could. Very embarrassed, he lifted the cover a little bit, stuck his ear out and listened, but luckily Meghan was still very much under the sheet and must have missed it. With great relief he let the air out of his lungs. That was close!

He tried to concentrate and resumed his crawl down to her feet. He desperately tried to find her toes, to have a taste of them, but for some strange reason he could not find them.

Shifting the cover again, he stuck his head outside, as it was getting very warm underneath. When he briefly put his head back under in search of her feet, he caught some sort of familiar but unexpected smell.

'Honey, can you please put your legs outside the covers? I want to feel every inch of you.'

Meghan did so, putting Harry into a trance.

'Ahh, Meghan, I can hardly contain myself; you are so sexy!' With a last attempt to hide his excitement, he uttered something like 'slippery when wet' and started to really dive into her sensational body.

But with a sudden cry, Harry found himself sitting upright in bed, completely confused.

'Darling, what's going on?' Meghan was wondering innocently if this cry was already the end of it.

'I ... I don't know, it's just ... your feet ... Meghan, did you ... did you really ... put your wellies on?' Harry stammered nervously.

'Well, erm, I, I ... I thought they are so sexy, and all of you Brits seem to love them; on almost every occasion you put on your wellies, and I started to find them so sexy too!'

Harry was beginning to understand the unexpected smell, and, not very amused, he started to pull the boots off Meghan. But now a sudden cry emerged from her mouth and she sat upright herself.

'What are you doing?' Meghan pleaded.

'Hell, Meghan, I just want to take off your boots. I don't think they actually belong here.'

Meghan whimpered.

'What's wrong, Meghie hearty?' Harry asked.

'Oh, Harry, I'm so insecure ...'

'About what? About what we're going to do?'

'No, about my feet ... unfortunately they are always so cold ... covering them in a pair of warm, sexy boots seemed like a good idea.'

Harry remembered the touch of her feet back in Canada, and she was right; she didn't seem to have the best circulation in her extremities. He had definitely cuddled with hotter women's feet in his life. He lifted his eyebrows; maybe it was indeed not the best idea to get the boots off. He refrained from pulling them off and, now that all doubts had been cleared, he started to love Meghan with all the delicious textures she offered him.

The Roast Chicken

Harry was again very nervous. He had heard from mutual friends that Meghan was an excellent cook, and, since she had pampered him with exquisite self-cooked treats, he could confirm her skills with his own tasting. He was very impressed by her creativity, which seemed to flow from her beautiful hands without effort. Hence, the pressure to keep up with her standard grew. As the days went by, he felt an increasing sense that he should introduce her to some real traditional English recipes.

He consulted a variety of websites and participated in a number of online discussions, naturally without unveiling his true identity. There he learnt a lot about the wisdom of housewives, and before long the grand day when he could show off his cooking skills came. He felt secure enough to avoid any awkward questions and was finally ready to contact the real expert. He decided to call Camilla.

He hoped it was the right moment to contact her, knowing very well that catching her at a bad time could be disastrous. Camilla could be very moody, and when that was the case it was better for any man not to be in close range. His father Charles could tell a story or two about that.

Harry picked up the phone and dialled the number of Clarence House.

*

Charles took his hat from the wardrobe, not being sure whether it would rain later on or not. The only thing he was sure of was that his stroll might take a few hours. The air in Clarence House was thick and, in his experience, it could take some time for Camilla to calm down. Therefore, he would prefer to clear her radar line.

He was generally a man of cheerful nature and a kind of easiness surrounded him in these relatively early hours of a Sunday. Nothing managed to frighten him any more after all he had experienced with women through his life; he was quite resistant against female terror.

He stopped, took another sip from the whisky flask he carried with him and continued his walk through the Wellington Arch and Hyde Park towards the grounds of Kensington Palace, whistling happily.

*

'Of course, Camilla. I will write that down with an exclamation mark. I don't know how to thank you for letting me take advantage of your years of experience roasting an outstanding chicken. Everybody in the family knows you are the best royal roaster! I owe you a debt of gratitude. Thank you indeed for sharing your knowledge with me; I appreciate it so much! Bye, Camilla, and have a restful and cheerful Sunday.'

Harry put down the phone, his cheeks flushed with anticipation. Now he was reassured he would be able to give Meghan a really good demonstration, not having to hide behind her high standard.

He rushed into the kitchen and started to whirl around the cooking island in the centre. He nearly threw some tools on the floor in his hectic, excited movements. At that moment, Meghan came through the door, singing, 'Harry, my dear Hairy, what are you up to?' to a cheerful melody.

*

As Charles approached Nottingham Cottage, a wonderful smell hung in the air. He put his nose in the air, sniffing intensely, trying to locate the source of the smell. For a second or two, he shivered, as the smell reminded him of Camilla's home. Was he somehow still in the surroundings of Clarence House? His heart came to an abrupt stop. Standing still and regaining consciousness, he realised that, for goodness' sake, it was just an illusion and he was strolling through the grounds of Kensington Palace. He sighed with relief, took another big sip of the whisky and continued his walk, getting quicker and quicker, trying to follow the smell.

The smell led him around a corner and behind a few bushes, and suddenly he stood in front of Nottingham Cottage, looking at the door, to which Meghan had fixed a lovely welcoming spray of flowers. It clearly marked that a woman had moved into the house.

Charles smiled. He was fond of Meghan. Not only did she bring a breath of fresh air into the royal family, but she enabled a new side to shine on his son. In the last few days, Charles had recognised a bustling activity and nervousness in Harry he knew only new lovers would have.

A romantic glow passed through Charles's eyes as he thought about his own past and falling in love. A quick picture of young Camilla appeared in his mind and a great wave of shock put him instantly back into the present. For God's sake, it was only a memory and Camilla was far away at the moment. Charles nervously dug around in his breast pocket, grabbed the flask and flushed down another long drink. This immediately put him back at ease and he felt calm and comfortable, a pleasant warmth flowing through his veins.

He stretched his hand towards the door, ready to knock, but at the last instant decided to pull it back and instead surprise the lovebirds with an unexpected visit. He carefully tried the door handle, which turned quite smoothly without making any noise and allowed Charles easy entry to the narrow hallway.

In the meantime, the chicken was gaining a nice bronze colour, but the couple were not quite sure whether the bird was done well enough. Harry was searching for a thermometer to measure the inside heat of the chicken and finally found one.

Charles quietly started to walk down the corridor. He paused as he heard Meghan's voice from the kitchen. Charles just stood there and listened.

'You want to stick it in?'

'Yeah, sure. I have been waiting for this moment for a long time,' Harry said with a moaning, vibrating voice.

'How does it feel?' Meghan asked. 'Is it juicy enough?'

'Oh, yeah, it is perfectly juicy and tender. The stick just glides in so easily. Ahh.'

'Don't you wanna push it in a bit further?'

'I just didn't want to push it all the way through to the other side.'

'No, it's fine, just keep going. Yes, just like that.'

Charles did not know where to go or what to think. He should not have just entered the house. There was definitely something going on he was not supposed to witness. What if he had to sneeze? What if the wooden floor gave away his presence?

Harry was preparing to pull the thermometer out of the chicken.

'Yes, I think you can take it out quickly,' Meghan said. 'Why don't you put it in from the other side too?'

'Do you really want to do it from both sides?'

'Sure, let's do it from both sides.'

Harry checked the temperature. 'OK, I'll take it out and then let's do the other side.'

'Good. Oh, Harry, how I look forward to swallowing the first juicy bit.' A sigh mingled with a groan left Meghan's lips.

Charles buried his head in his hands, not knowing where to look or what to do. He had not expected such action in the kitchen, nor had he had any intention of intruding on a scene not meant for his ears or eyes. Now he stood trapped in his son's place with no escape in sight. Too anxious to risk making any treacherous sound, Charles remained where he was.

'Let me just take a sip of the juice,' Meghan said.

'Don't just swallow it so quickly; you can't taste it properly like that.'

'I did taste it; it tastes so wonderful.'

'We must put it back in now.'

'Let me touch it gently again,' Meghan said. 'Mm, nice, but it is still a little soft. I think we should get it a little harder on the outside while trying to keep the juice inside. Well, what if I take a bite? What do you think?'

'Oh, Meghan, it's too early to take a bite. It's so delicate, you might destroy it.'

Two sudden cries escaped from the kitchen, Charles

standing paralysed in the entrance hall. He heard some panting, his feet being pulled closer to the thin kitchen door, which stood open only half an inch: enough to allow some sound out, but not offering a glimpse of what was going on behind it. Through his near-panic, Charles's bladder started to send emergency signals after his high consumption of alcoholic treats, which didn't help his rising unease.

'Let me have another drop of juice, then,' Meghan said, before crying out again. 'Ouch, I think I might burn my mouth, it's so hot!'

'Of course it's hot; what did I tell you?' Harry demanded. 'I told you to be careful! What if I drip some cream over it to make it juicier?'

'Well, that's a good idea. I like it when it's creamy.' There was a pause, and then Meghan spoke again, almost groaning. 'Oh, yes, pour it all over it . . .'

With one hand Meghan opened the oven; with the other she pointed to the chicken ready in the roasting pot. 'Now get it back in again. It's cooled down too much already. Can you give me a hand, please?'

'With pleasure; it's high time to get it back in now,' Harry said. A moment passed. 'Be careful. No, Meghan, what are you doing, we need to shove it in slowly!'

Harry was panting. By this point Charles's ears were deep purple. He started to count the flowers on the tapestry.

Silence. Some noise of effort and painful pushing action escaped from the kitchen. Panting again ... heavy breathing ...

This was too much for Charles. In a quick movement of despair, he put his hand into his pocket, and the sudden touch of the rubber material inside gave him instant hope. What a good idea to always be prepared for the worst situation! Charles sighed and a faint smile brushed over his lips.

Another loud cry brought his attention back to what was going on in the kitchen. He frowned.

'Come on, Harry, just push it a little further inside!'

'Like that?'

'No, the position is no good yet; I'll give you a hand and we'll do it together.'

Harry and Meghan both grabbed some oven gloves and kitchen towels, trying to reposition the chicken in the hot steamy oven. Heavy breathing; their breathing got louder and quickened.

In a common act of exhaustion, Harry and Meghan cried out together at once.

'For heaven's sake, finally!' Harry exclaimed. 'Now it's inside and perfectly positioned for a good final roasting. Let's get the heat up and accelerate the process.'

'How long shall we keep it going?' Meghan asked.

'A few more minutes, surely.'

'Super; this is roasting to perfection!'

A close aeroplane taking off made it impossible for Charles to continue listening to the ongoing conversation. He had to wait a few minutes until the noise faded out.

Charles moved closer to the door, until his feet touched the wood of it, and he pressed his large ear on the surface to work like a satellite dish when another aeroplane made hearing difficult again.

Harry was saying something. 'Let me take off my ... I am so hot and sweaty ...'

Harry had started to prepare the sauce for the bird, chopping veggies, squeezing lemons.

Charles could hear a rhythmic noise coming from the kitchen. It sounded as if some cloth were being swept over a tile.

'Why are you doing this?' Meghan demanded. 'This won't add to the process!'

'Surely it will add something!' Harry exclaimed. 'Camilla told me that I should do this! Well, at least she should know from years of experience!'

Oh, heavens! Charles pressed his eyes shut, a pained expression on his fallen face. Camilla! Why did she pursue him everywhere and torture him pitilessly? His shaky hand slowly approached the bottle. But an abrupt sound interrupted his plan.

Meghan moaning again . . .

'Are you sure we should do this?' Meghan asked. 'It's so strange . . . well, I haven't done it before; it is very strenuous!'

'I know, darling, but it is absolutely needed for a good result,' Harry assured her. 'We have to turn it round and get it done from the other side as well.'

'Jesus, I am getting out of breath, it's so slippery. Don't pull so much; you should push more!'

'More?' Harry asked. 'I can try . . .'

In a flurry of mutual panting, the cries built up more and more until they collapsed in a common climax, and the additional noise of a kind of explosion from the kitchen nearly swept Charles off his feet. He could hardly stay upright, gasping for air. This was the end!

In a last desperate attempt to get a grip, he fell down on his knees, steered his hand into his pocket and in a rush of anxiety blew into the tube of the rubber ring. The rubber expanded and, with great relief, Charles realised that his effort was not in vain. Very content, he looked at his inflated rescue tool.

After a couple of minutes, Harry opened the oven, took out the hot chicken and asked Meghan to put some cork underlays on the wooden surface. He cried out, 'It is so incredibly hot, I can't hold it for much longer.'

'Just hold on a bit. I'm coming,' Meghan said, her voice accelerating. 'I'm almost there.'

And with a very high-pitched voice she continued, 'Just hold it.'

And finally she screamed out with vehemence, 'I'm coming, I'm coming.'

Meghan was in a rush to cover the workplace with some underlays and was panting at double rate.

When Meghan was ready, she shouted, 'You can come now; just don't drip it all over the floor.'

Pulling together his last strength, Harry stumbled over, roaring with despair, 'I'm coooming . . .' and placed the bird on the underlays.

After a few minutes, when his quickened breathing had calmed down, he said, 'Do you want to have another taste of juice now?' He grabbed a spoon.

'Oh, yes, I can't get enough satisfaction,' Meghan said, with a big smile on her face.

Harry took a spoonful of the sauce from the bowl and directed it to Meghan's mouth.

'It tastes so wonderfully spicy,' Meghan said. 'It's so warm and creamy.'

'I am glad you like it. You make me so proud. Let it cool down a bit before swallowing.'

A moment passed before Harry spoke again.

'Oh, Meghan, that was the best collaboration I've ever had. You really gave everything, I have to say. It was extraordinary teamwork. I am so proud of you!'

'Oh, Harry. You are the best! And this creamy juice is the best I have ever tasted.'

Hardly able to pull himself together, Charles hurried upstairs, knowing that relief would come to him in seconds.

Inside the bathroom, Charles opened the button on his creased trousers and with a nervous gesture flipped the toilet cover open, placed his inflatable toilet seat over the installed wooden one and finally found relief.

'God save the Queen, and myself. That was close!'

After taking a few minutes to calm down, Charles managed to open the air valve without great noise, put the folded rubber seat back into the inside pocket of his jacket and sneaked down, trying to escape without being noticed.

In the kitchen, heavy steam billowed through the opening of the door, giving the situation a grotesque note. A smell of roasted flesh spread in the cottage. Charles sped up, hurrying to get out of there.

In that moment, the kitchen door flew open and an astonished Harry, his hair wild, sweat sweeping over his face and red cheeks, wearing only underpants and holding a fork with a juicy piece of roast chicken on it, looked at Charles.

'Pa, what are you doing here?'

'That's what I thought I should ask you,' Charles replied, blushing like a teenager ...

The Baptism

At Clarence House, Charles was known for being pedantic about keeping his garden organic; after all, he had a reputation of leading organic farming to defend. Therefore, no insecticides were to be sprayed, no pesticides to be applied, no artificial fertilisers to be used, no slug poison to be spread. A whole bunch of gardeners were employed to pull up every weed by hand. To keep the flowers free from slugs, each slug had to be picked up by hand and put into a basket and brought away.

Work happened especially during the night, with head-mounted torches, so Camilla would be able to have her stroll during the day without bumping into staff all the time. Of nothing else was Charles more afraid than enraging his wife. He loved her very much and tried to please her in every way he was able.

When Harry heard about the deportation of the slugs, he was furious with his father, blaming him of risking the lives of all these innocent creatures. Harry had a golden heart and loved everything that was alive on this planet, from plants to insects to animals to human beings. He had inherited his sense of humanity from his beloved late mother. A charitable attitude had somehow been laid into his cradle and he had a natural way of displaying it. Therefore, deporting slugs in closed containers across large distances in an attempt to tame nature was something he completely disapproved of.

Harry felt pity for these lovely creatures and, without telling his father, he had instructed the gardeners to bring them over to Nottingham Cottage in order to reduce travel distance to a minimum and let them free there. Harry thought that from there they could find their own way and crawl to wherever they wanted to live. The grounds of Kensington Palace were tremendous and there were enough bushes and plants for them to live on.

What he failed to notice was that the slugs increasingly started to populate his small garden. Some of their favourite flowers were growing there, ones the slugs adored above anything, and this reduced their appetite for long-distance travel.

Harry was rarely in his garden. He was so busy, and recently, with Meghan filling his life, he was even busier. Everywhere in the garden, slimy tracks could be seen, and during the night the slugs even started to climb up the walls and enter the windows which were kept open for fresh air.

*

Meghan did not want to get married without having been baptised beforehand. As she had not been baptised as a child, she was keen to get this done now.

The baptism ceremony was approaching with big steps and put Meghan in an ever-growing state of anxiety. She was very nervous about new customs in the Anglican Church and that she could make a fatal mistake during the ceremony. Almost every week she had to go to the nail studio for new artificial nails because she was biting them off due to nervousness. What she told Harry was that she was excited to try out all the cool British nail colours in her new homeland.

She was reading books and looking for information about Anglican customs on the internet, but it was difficult to find much. Meghan was ultra-nervous, picturing the Archbishop of Canterbury standing in front of her like a huge saint, raising his hand in order to baptise her while the gathered royal family watched.

She therefore decided to secretly practise for this important event.

Time was running quicker than she would have liked as the day approached and Harry was not often out without her. He was almost glued to her, so keen was he to spend every single moment with his newfound sweetheart. Meghan was very much in love with hairy Harry, but for her current undertaking he was totally unwelcome.

There was only one day when he was due out, and she had to take advantage of that. What made things a little more complicated was that her most trusted butler was on leave on precisely the same day. She would have to rely on the newly employed Romanian girl who could hardly speak any English.

Meghan was a sly girl and knew that the upcoming ceremony involved water being poured over one's head. To avoid any tracks in the house, she decided to go out in the garden to practise for the procedure.

In a moment of heavenly inspiration, Meghan had the idea to wear a newly acquired pair of wellies to avoid getting wet. She didn't favour the idea of getting a splash of cold water on her usually cold feet. In England the temperatures were unfortunately different to where she had been brought up. Full of pride, she pulled on the very shiny boots that she had not worn before. Being a bit superstitious, she thought shiny wellies might help to make her shine in the new phase of her life for which she was preparing. To underline the virginity of the process, the boots were white.

The sun was just about to rise when Meghan got hold of the Romanian girl and led her into the garden. This required a great deal of energy and body language. It was still twilight, and it was therefore easy to miss that the garden was packed with wandering slugs. These animals loved the fresh and damp ground of early mornings or late evenings.

Meghan had brought a small bowl of warm water to be used for the training. She had already placed it on the bench before bringing her assistant outside. Meghan was proud of herself, and her own organisational talent put her into a state of ecstasy.

She explained to her helper in the simplest of words what she was going to expect from her. Meghan was gesturing wildly while saying the words 'you' and 'water' and pointing at her own head. She finally managed to bring the girl to shyly nod her head, which gave Meghan the conviction that she must have understood all of it.

All was good and Meghan finally took her position, standing on a freshly slimed spot, folding her hands, closing her eyes and saying a prayer in her mind. As an actress she knew that an authentic role always needed real emotions and gestures to underline the impression of genuineness.

Meghan prayed. And prayed. And prayed. And nothing happened. She continued to pray. And still nothing happened.

After an apparent eternity had passed, she dared to open the lid of one eye just enough to peep out and see what was going on. To her utmost dismay, her imagined priestess had taken a seat on the nearby bench and was examining her long pink fingernails.

Meghan was furious and instantly forgot that she had just spent minutes murmuring the sweetest prayers. Within a second, she opened both eyes and yelled in a very high pitch, 'What the hell are you doing? Pour water over my head!' She pointed exaggeratedly at her head. 'Water on head!' she repeated, to make herself unmistakably clear.

The girl had sunk into deep thoughts of her boyfriend, who was back in Romania, when Meghan's sudden shouting made her jump in her seat. She was so shocked and horrified that she grabbed the nearest watering can.

Instantaneously, shock hit Meghan as the water touched her and she was frozen in action, standing there like a statue. The water was very fresh and cold, close to freezing. This had not been foreseen in her plan.

After another seeming eternity had passed, the water having spilled completely over her head, dripping down her face and body and into the newly purchased wellies, a cry of incomparable misery shook the whole garden of Nottingham Cottage. The fake priestess was quick to flee from the garden, closely followed by Meghan.

It took a long time for Meghan to recover from that cold shock. Standing wailing under the warm cascade of the shower in the bathroom, flushed with self-pity, she tried to think of how she could wash away this bad memory.

After the hot shower, rolled up in a thick layer of

towels, Meghan set her brain to high speed, conjuring up a new plan.

Full of self-confidence, she called her temporary butler and made her way back to the garden, pulling the reluctant girl along behind her by the hand. How could her brilliant plan ever have been allowed to fail?

This time, Meghan had thought of every small detail. She had put on her bikini and was now wearing thick woollen socks in the wellies, had donned her snorkel for breathing purposes, and had put very warm – almost boiling – water into the watering can and any other canister in the garden. What could go wrong now?

With enormous patience she placed her helper close to her, handed her the watering can and closed her eyes again. Meghan started her prayer with all her heart; she put every single possible feeling into the prayer. And she prayed.

The utterly frightened lady butler, afraid to make another mistake, took the watering can, lifted it up and started tipping it while Meghan introduced another silent prayer. In that very moment, the priestess noticed that a slug was wandering up her hand, having just come out of the watering can. This time, the yell that interrupted proceedings came out of the Romanian's mouth. She immediately let the can fall down, which made an enormous bang just seconds after the cry.

Meghan thought that maybe the end of the world was coming and started to join the crying. This in turn provoked the girl to cry louder.

Meghan was so horrified that, half in a trance, her mind still in silent prayer, she started to step back. Behind her, moist from the spilled water, the slimy tracks of the slugs made the terrain more slippery. With a movement close to an ice skater on her first day, flailing helplessly with her arms, Meghan lost balance and fell backwards into a brier. This electrified her with another shock, screaming even louder.

Her unlucky helper suddenly leapt from paralysed shock into action. Thinking that Meghan was being bitten by slugs in the bush, she took the nearby hose and fully opened the cold water tap. Her eyes pressed together, the girl with a last effort of despair managed to wash down poor Meghan from head to toe, the pressure of the water forcing Meghan even deeper into the thorny brier. Due to the rush of water the girl couldn't tell whether Meghan's screaming or her own yelling was louder.

Needless to say, Meghan certainly did not give up just because of this admittedly disastrous incident. For many years she had been a proud member of the feminist movement, and she refused to accept that, with at least one intelligent woman present, they were not capable of fulfilling this simple and necessary task.

One thing, though, did torture her mind: something she absolutely could not make sense of. This was the girl's answer when Meghan had asked where all these slugs were coming from. The girl had just said, 'Harry bring,' much to Meghan's disapproval. She swore to question Harry about this and, if needed, to take revenge on him.

*

Prince Philip was in a very good mood that morning. The sun was starting to shine and inspiration hit him on mornings like these. He had taken a turn to Nottingham Cottage, not having strolled over there for quite some time. His nose lifted up in the air; he smelled the wonderful scent of flowers, the bees humming in the air, and suddenly two female voices caught his attention.

He approached slowly, not being sure where the voices came from. Stopping and setting his hearing aid to full volume, he was able to make out that the sounds were coming from the garden at Nottingham Cottage. With a big smile he walked over to the fence, trying to spot something through the thick hedge.

The sight he caught there made his eyes widen. Standing there in a full-body diving suit was Meghan, with snorkel, goggles and wellies. Strangely enough, Meghan was even wearing a helmet, which gave the scene a grotesque note. Next to her was a girl who made a very insecure impression, wearing ear protection and dressed in wax clothes. Unfortunately, he was not able to hear their conversation. Then Meghan pressed her hands together as if in prayer and the girl, closing her eyes, seemingly whispered a prayer to herself.

Prince Philip frowned, swallowed quickly and raised his voice, which was trained from the army to jump to very loud intonation from a standstill. With the immediacy of approaching thunder he cried out, 'Is this a fertility ritual? Can I join in?' He was already bouncing on his feet with excitement.

Even with helmet and ear protection, it hit the ladies with the impact of cannon fire.

The two girls broke out into uncontrollable screaming and yelling, which made all three participants flee in different directions.

At Buckingham Palace

Today, Meghan was completely on her own, with Harry out performing some army duties she couldn't possibly join him for. She didn't mind. Everything was so fresh and she was curious to explore her new surroundings.

Harry had asked for permission for Meghan to visit Buckingham Palace, and permission had been granted. She liked the adventure and the thought of being able to explore at least parts of this imposing palace on her own.

After a brief introduction, she was allowed one hour of self-guided touring inside the palace. She was over-whelmed by the architecture, the old paintings and artwork, the richness of the interior and the splendid grandeur that emanated from every inch of stone and fabric. The magnificence of bygone times and ancient kingdoms lay in the air. Never had she seen anything similar; not even her visits to Washington, DC, and the White House had been that impressive. With open mouth she ambled silently through the corridors, trying to absorb the tingling atmosphere with every breath she took. She felt like a princess in a castle, which she kind of was anyway.

Outside, it was a bright and sunny day, which meant that a lot of doors and windows were left open to let some fresh air in. Meghan was glad, as she thoroughly disapproved of the musty and stale odour some old buildings would produce. Her sense of smell was very developed and for emergency situations she always carried an air freshener in her handbag.

On days like these, the staff were a little less strict and stiff and often could be found in the inner yard, smoking a cigarette or having a chat.

Meghan was totally on her own when she strolled down a wide and particularly ornamented corridor that passed a large double door. A distinct conversation behind the slightly open door caught her attention. The door seemed heavy and thick, its highly embellished decoration suggesting that it led into a special room.

She managed to get closer without interrupting the ongoing conversation. She was able to clearly make out the Queen's voice and a male voice she couldn't place. Their conversation seemed very lively, and she edged closer still to listen better to what was going on.

Meghan did not know that the Queen was having a conversation with her Lord Chamberlain. They were talking about the upcoming visit of Germany's Chancellor, Mrs Angela Merkel.

'Oh, do you?' The Queen laughed. 'I think we will manage her visit, although I have to let you know, I am not very amused after the latest incidents.'

Meghan frowned, getting closer, her designer shoes touching the antique wooden frame of the door. She tucked her hair behind her ears, allowing them to be wide open.

'Well, you know,' the Queen was saying, 'it is always difficult with foreigners. They come to our land, don't know about our customs, speak terrible English, and we still have to pretend to be close friends.'

The other voice said something that Meghan couldn't catch, making her even more curious.

The Queen spoke again. 'This lady in particular dresses very unfavourably. To be honest, I don't like her style at all, but that is not the only thing about Mrs Merkel ...'

The pipe band practising on the lawn made it difficult to make out each word clearly, but Meghan was quite sure she had heard the Queen say her last name. Oh, goodness, that was her name, Markle; the Queen was talking about her! Meghan swallowed, her eyes enlarging.

Nervously she got hold of the wall's exquisite tapestry, trying to find support to battle her rising unease. At the same time anger was rising in her; they seemed incapable of even pronouncing her name correctly, and yet the Queen claimed that foreigners didn't speak proper English! Meghan was boiling with rage.

Meghan remembered how Harry had repeatedly told her that the Queen was to be addressed as *ma'am*, and that this was pronounced *'ma'am* as in *ham*, not *ma'am* as in *farm'*. Did the Queen think that it was *Merkle* as in *gherkin*, as opposed to *Markle* as in *sparkle*?

It was definitely the Queen who was wrong. *I already corrected the faults of a large chemical company when I was nine years old; I am now going to set the Queen straight*, Meghan told herself.

The Lord Chamberlain replied, 'Yes, Mrs Merkel really dresses in a very old-fashioned way, I have to admit, ma'am.'

'Oh, and that is not the only thing: her English, oh my God. Sometimes I can hardly understand what she's trying to say.'

This was too much for Meghan. The Queen had made herself unmistakably clear. Obviously, she found Meghan's style old-fashioned and did not like her English.

Meghan was at a loss; this was very tough news for her. But at the same time, she swore to take revenge for being attacked in such an unfair way. Her sweet heart was broken.

She bent her head and started walking back up the corridor, trying to be as invisible as when she had come.

Meghan was very sad. But, after a few minutes, hope stirred again. Yes, she was capable of bringing the Queen to her side.

Meghan decided to alter her attire and work on her American accent. In the former part of her life she had been able to confront any kind of seemingly unmanageable hardship and master the challenge. After all, she was an actress, and what a re-MARK-ab-LE one! From now on, she would indeed act. She would use all of her acting talent to silence any and all critics in the entire kingdom, once and for all.

Meghan strolled happily out of the palace, drawing up some of the changes she was planning to implement. She would demonstrate at the earliest occasion, in front of the whole gathered royal family, what complete immaculateness meant!

Back at Nottingham Cottage, she decided to call her new best friend.

She dialled the number of Victoria Beckham.

Dinner for More Than One

Finally, the day came when Meghan could prove to the last doubter that she had adapted perfectly to what was expected from her and could sweep away even the smallest questioning thought. The Queen had invited her to Buckingham Palace for a dinner to welcome Meghan Markle as a future member of the royal family.

Meghan had been in earnest preparation for weeks already. Nobody had a clue as to what exactly she was up to, though, not even Harry. She would only engage in her preparations when he was away. Every time, she carefully reassured herself that absolutely nobody was in the cottage and suspiciously watched Harry from the upstairs window until he had disappeared around the corner. Even then, she still waited for a few more minutes, listening intently, in case he realised he had forgotten something and returned unexpectedly. Only when she was totally sure that all was good would she speed downstairs, close all windows and lock the front door to be completely on her own. Now she had time to practise.

She went upstairs again, closed the curtains and ceremoniously opened her wardrobe. All the way in the back, she had managed to make an undetectable space where she was hiding a few clothes. One day she had gone to a costume shop to get equipped. Out of the wardrobe she brought a second-hand dress covered with old-fashioned flowers in a granny-like rose colour. Her nose wrinkled at the awful smell of stale fabric as the dress had hung for too long in a musty back room. Goodness, how she had to suffer to carve her place in the royal family.

Putting her mind into trained acting mode, she very professionally put the smelly clothes on. She had deliberately not washed the clothes, because – awfully enough – the stench was useful. As an actress she was accustomed to doing things that she didn't like but were essential for the part. More importantly, dressing appropriately helped her mind get into the desired role.

She opened the squeaking door of the bathroom and sneaked in. To prevent even any possible rat in the house from getting involved in what was going on, she closed the door behind her.

She stood in front of the mirror, looking at herself. Then she started to let her mind drift away, imagining a very traditional, elderly and stiff British woman. She took quite a lot of time, until she saw this woman very sharply in her mind, letting herself sink emotionally into how such a person must have felt. To underline the process, she grabbed the horrible auntie hat she had bought at a flea market and put it on.

She looked into the mirror, stiffened her lip and, with a raised voice, started trying to speak the most British upper-class English she could imagine. She added a lot of remarks like 'Reeeeally,' 'Oh, no,' 'Oh, yes,' 'Oh, do you?' and so on, just as she had observed during several ladies' conversations in the last few months.

Talking to herself, she started to take on the mannerisms that such conversations usually included, and the longer she trained, the easier it was for her. She repeated the process until she felt safe and, strangely enough, almost started to like it.

She was on the verge of taking it too far. One day, when she and Harry were sitting on the sofa, in the middle of a very relaxed conversation, Meghan answered with her well-trained granny-style English. Harry was utterly shocked, looking at her with wide eyes, not understanding what was going on. Quickly, Meghan cleared her throat, changed the subject and hoped he would forget about it as quickly as it had happened. From then on, she was more cautious.

The next thing for Meghan to address was the way she dressed. Her rosy clothes were essential for training her English accent, but she would never wear them in front of other people, especially after the Queen had criticised her for looking frumpy. She searched for a bundle she was hiding in her wardrobe. Her hands grabbed the bag and she took out a few garments. While caressing the soft and silky material she started to warm up inside. It felt so sexy and feminine. Yeah, this was the right stuff to show the Queen! With it returned her self-esteem and her dignity.

She was so glad that Victoria Beckham had been able to deliver some extravagant outfits. Luckily, Vicky still had some really good examples of what 'sexy style' actually meant from her former time on stage as a Spice Girl. This would be spot on.

*

Before long, the day of the grand dinner arrived. It was getting late and Harry was impatient. Where was Meghan? Harry had returned from an officers' meeting and gone straight to Buckingham Palace. All of the guests were already seated, waiting for his fiancée. This was not good. Harry's feet started to shuffle under the large table.

Grouped around the festively decorated banquet table were his father Charles with Camilla, his brother William with Kate and of course the Queen and Prince Philip, along with about another dozen couples. Still no Meghan visible. Harry's hairy toes were starting to cramp up.

Suddenly, some rising excitement could be heard in the hallway, suggesting something special was on the way. Harry heard a few whispers and sounds he could not place. His anticipation and nervousness grew.

Everybody was sitting silently, the silence murdering Harry. It was so embarrassing.

Finally, the butler opened the door and in came Meghan. But what on earth was she wearing? Just a quick glance was almost enough to make Harry faint. Oh, goodness! And the way she greeted everybody? Was he hearing it correctly, this mannered and over-accentuated British accent? Harry's toes were whirling by this point; he could hardly control his feet any more.

Sitting down, Meghan brimmed with self-confidence, throwing her made-up hair back. What in God's name had she done with her hair? Harry's eyes were nearly exploding. She was wearing a beehive which could easily have competed with that of the late Amy Winehouse.

The Queen cleared her throat while everybody was shifting uncomfortably in their seats, and she finally gave the sign to commence the dinner procedure. Plates were quickly served. This was the opportunity for Harry to quickly send a glance to Meghan, whispering under his beard, 'Where have you been, Meg?'

But, unfortunately, the silence was back after the clatter of serving and Harry had to continue his groping in the dark.

After a few minutes the Queen placed her soup spoon down on the table: signal enough for everybody to mirror her behaviour, exactly as protocol demanded. Except for Meghan. She continued to move the spoon absently between the plate and her heavily made-up red lips. The scene brought to mind the performance of a lone piper, but one was on purpose and graceful; the other was not. Meghan did not understand how alone she was in this moment as she went on eating, proudly sporting her long, cat-like red nails. Harry's sight started to blur as he wished he were in Scotland and Meghan a piper.

A harrumphing didn't help to bring Meghan's attention to what was going on. The female guests at the dinner looked down in embarrassment into their mostly empty plates; the men stared helplessly at the ceiling and the walls, trying to find relief in distraction. Everybody tried to avoid the unavoidable and inescapable situation, except for the Queen. Her eyes were fixed upon Meghan, and her otherwise pale face started to get pinkish in response to being totally ignored.

Harry had to do something, but he could only make a despairing effort to contact Meghan under the table. He took all his self-control and directed a very pointed hit with his shoes in Meghan's direction. He had not taken into account that Prince Philip liked stretching his long legs under the table, and he thudded fully into his grandfather's feet. Philip jumped nervously in his seat, thinking it was his wife who had given him a sign. As Philip opened his mouth, Harry recognised his mistake just in time and quickly blurted out, 'So nice here,' giving Philip a meaningful glance.

Harry was in terror of Philip making one of the sharp remarks he was well known for. It would be the end if his grandfather directly spoke what everybody was merely thinking. Harry's feet were wet from perspiration by this time.

Meghan hadn't noticed what was going on at all, and, to make things worse, she started to have a conversation with her neighbour, Prince Charles. The only sounds in the large dining room were the scratching of Meghan's cutlery and her far too accentuated speech.

Everybody except Harry was in great shock. Harry was beyond great shock. He was hallucinating an army rescue by this point.

To finally obtain the required respect, the Queen took her dessert spoon and rapped it against her empty dessert wine glass to call for a toast. This immediately took everybody out of their reverie. Even Meghan stopped her boombox-like exaggerated laughter and put aside her wet and red lipstick-soaked spoon.

When the staff cleared the table for the second serving, Harry was finally able to speak a few words to Meghan. 'Meghan, what's this outfit? What happened to your voice? What's going on?'

But, before she was able to respond, the next course was being served.

Every new course was torture for Harry. He was just so helpless, unable to control this situation, while everybody was trying to put on a good face for this impossible evening. It was a nightmare.

Thankfully, Meghan was still seated and only her upper

part visible. Her entry had been so quick that no one had had a chance to take in her entire outfit. Harry was sure this would be different at the end of the dinner when she left the table. He remembered from his quick glimpse when she had entered that she had been wearing a miniskirt which was far more than daring, stockings like a pole dancer and high heels which were sure to make the wearer as well as any onlooker giddy. For now, only her lace bra could be spotted beneath her wildly open blouse.

Harry's throat was as dry as his drinking glass. He almost grabbed the flower vase to get a sip of the water, such was his state of desperation.

'Mmay ai excuuse myselff? I havve to gou to the laydies,' Meghan announced in terribly exaggerated English.

Everybody appeared to be looking forward to a few minutes of relief, a break from the horror show that was going on. Meghan stood up with such abrupt power that her chair almost fell over, with Harry managing to get hold of it at the last second.

It took Meghan an eternity to rise onto her never-ending high heels. Everybody was fidgeting while she continued to show her broadest smile, red lipstick everywhere on her bleached teeth. Harry was frozen, while his feet were steaming by now. With a very sexy swing, Meghan turned and set off towards the door.

This can't be happening, Harry thought to himself. *You should never, ever turn your back to the Queen.*

For a moment it was all black in front of his eyes. By the time he had recovered, Meghan was out of sight.

With a common sigh, everybody sank a little deeper into their chairs, but unexpectedly the door flew open again and in came Meghan with wagging hips, purring, 'Oh, I forgot my clutch.' She giggled awkwardly.

This was his chance! Harry gave Meghan a clear and unmistakable glance and indicated that she should leave the room backwards. Meghan's face fell; how could she have forgotten when the event was going so perfectly?

With an awkward movement she faced the Queen, her smile not so innocent any more, and started to walk backwards. She overlooked the chair that was still standing behind her, and with a very loud and very unladylike movement she stumbled over it, falling backwards. The last thing Harry saw was her legs up in the air, giving unhindered access to her suspender stockings and string thong, before his view faded completely.

When Harry opened his eyes again, he recognised Kate hovering beside him, fanning him with a napkin, and heard excited murmuring everywhere.

'Kate, where is Meghan?' was the only thing Harry was able to stammer through his dry lips.

'She's safe now. Calm down; everything will be all right,' she answered in a worried but trustworthy and motherly way.

Harry's eyes lost sight again.

The Screw-Up

Neither Meghan nor Harry had been able to participate in the second half of the dinner party the Queen had arranged for Meghan. All the mishaps were put down to Meghan having been too nervous and the number of dinner guests just too large.

Kate had come up with the idea to hold another dinner party for Meghan and Harry at their home at Anmer Hall. This time, the invitees were only the closest family members and the occasion was to be a very relaxed and informal one. Meghan was truly delighted to be given a second chance to shine. She allowed extra time to choose her outfit, following different advice this time, and changed her hairdresser, but she kept the tooth bleach she was using.

As they drove up the long drive of Anmer Hall, Meghan beamed at Harry, showing him her sweetest smile, Harry beamed back at her like an enlightened plum. Both of them were anxious to make a good impression.

Having had some starting problems over the pebbles with her vertiginous killer high heels, Harry and Meghan finally stood in front of the richly decorated entrance door with throbbing hearts. Meghan's delicate hand rang the bell.

From inside, decisive steps could be heard. After a swift turn of the handle, the heavy door flew open and William, brimming with joy, stood in the doorway. Meghan shivered.

In the car Harry had looked like a mature plum with his flushed face and red hair, and now William looked like a pear! What else was taking place tonight? Was this a fruit gathering? Or even a veggie party? Quick images flashed into her mind; Charles often had the look of a squeezed lemon, especially when his face lay in folds while laughing. Camilla's head sometimes emanated the air of a cauliflower and Prince Philip occasionally competed with asparagus. The Queen had been compared to a cabbage; her husband seemed convinced. And Kate? Meghan was not quite sure what she might resemble. A dry raisin, perhaps?

A slight insecurity caught Meghan while entering, as she was trying to find what her own place was within her newfound family. Somebody had once told her her cheeks had a similarity to puffed popcorn, which might technically be considered a vegetable, but she quickly forgot about that while being absorbed by greeting the other family members.

Meghan felt a bit tense, not wanting to make any kind of mistake, or at least not a big one like last time. At least her dress was not revealing anything it shouldn't.

Meghan was about to take the seat Kate had offered her when a sudden stir caught her attention. Looking around nervously, she noticed that William still stood at the entrance, while Harry was on the other side of the reception room, blocking the way to a sitting room. Everybody else was now sitting, except Kate, who was swirling around with the kids, and William and Harry, who were standing at the doors. Meghan didn't understand.

And then, with a very loud commanding voice that might be heard in the army, Harry shouted heartily through the room, 'Aaare the doors shut?'

William cried back from the entrance, 'Shuuttt!!' and a loud bang was heard.

In the rear of the reception room Harry shouted, 'Doooors shut!' and forcefully slammed the door. 'Aaarm the slides!'

William: 'Slides aaaarmed!'

'Slides aaaaarmed!' Harry trilled.

Prince Philip clicked his heels with excitement. 'Cross-check!' he shouted even louder, a roguish smile on his face.

William: 'OK, chrross-check dooone.'

Harry: 'OK, dooone.'

Prince Philip, with utmost enthusiasm: 'Faaasten seat belts!'

William, his voice cracking, tears running down his cheeks: 'Seaat belts faaastened!'

Harry's shout mingled with a chuckle. 'All belts faaastened!'

Prince Philip, brimming with roaring laughter: 'Ready for take-offfff.'

By this point Meghan was utterly shocked. Where was this leading? Where on earth had she landed? This was surely neither a fruit nor a veggie gathering. She felt she was being taken down the highway to hell.

Philip was by her side, slapping his thigh, barely able to speak while bursting out with laughter. 'You know, Meghan, Kate's parents … they were both flight attendants. We usually follow this procedure before everyone is seated – but of course only when the closest family is together!'

Kate rolled her eyes but let them have their giggle.

Once the adults had calmed down, William and Kate

were very busy trying to control George and Charlotte, who, inspired by the foolishness of the grown-ups, were both up for antics. Harry felt a strong need to lubricate his dry throat and approached Meghan to whisper in her ear. 'Come on, sweetie, let's go to the kitchen and get some drinks.'

While the hosts were occupied and Prince Philip was chatting with the Queen, Meghan rushed after Harry, glad to escape the grotesque scene she had just experienced.

*

Kate finally managed to calm down the siblings a bit, threatening to take them straight to bed if they didn't behave. This helped temporarily. Looking around, she noticed that Meghan and Harry were not present. She thought the lovebirds might have gone for a walk in the garden, and she decided to head for the kitchen to get some refreshments for the guests.

As she approached the kitchen, some strange sounds made her hesitate, and she stopped in the hallway and listened. She was almost sure that what she was hearing had to be Meghan's and Harry's voices. The loud conversation from the reception room made it difficult to hear and allowed only fragments of words to pass through the door. Kate approached the slightly open door a little bit more.

Inside the kitchen, Harry and Meghan were trying to open a bottle of wine. Harry hardly ever had to open a bottle himself, as he was a keen beer sipper, and at formal dinners he was usually served wine a butler had opened. Meghan, meanwhile, was not very experienced with bottles that had a real cork.

Kate heard Harry say, 'Before I start with the screwing, I have to make sure I place it right in the middle. You can help me with that.'

Kate's immaculate left eyebrow lifted a third of an inch.

'Meghan, hold the rim very firmly so it doesn't slip. Yeah, you're doing well, just carry on like that. Now I can start screwing very slowly.'

Kate's other eyebrow joined the first.

Meghan was providing some panting ...

'Meghan, it feels so tight, I can barely make it go in much further.'

'No, Harry, you are only about halfway in; you need to get in deeper. This is a rather young co ... k, and quite hard. I know they get softer with age.'

'OK, honey, let me push some more; we have to find the right rhythm to screw it deeper.'

Both Harry and Meghan seemed to breathe rhythmically together.

'I think it's now in as deep as possible. Oof, that was a tough one.'

Kate's mouth dropped open, while both eyebrows rose another third of an inch and her face started to get pale.

Harry spoke again. 'Meghan, take hold of both items at the side – be careful, they are delicate – and start pulling out slowly. Just nice and gentle. When I feel you get stuck, I'll drill it slightly back in, then please squeeze with both hands again. Don't press too hard. Just apply a nice rhythm. Before it gets out completely, hold it straight, so that it doesn't spill a drop.'

'Oh, Harry, this is so tough!'

The panting was interrupted by a cry from Meghan. Kate didn't know where to look; she almost fell when

William bumped into her. She put her forefinger on her lips, making her husband understand he was to be still.

Some heavy rhythmic noise was being heard inside and some squeaking, like when little Charlotte bobbed up and down in her child seat. William's eyes were getting bigger; he tried to suppress a laugh.

'You did really well, Meghan!' Harry exclaimed. 'Now let's do it again. Please help me by holding it right in the middle before I start drilling. Ready? I'll drill slowly, but surely.'

A moment passed before Harry spoke again. 'I am completely in now; we can now start pulling it out with the same rhythm as before.'

Again, the same squeaking sound made William and Kate freeze, their eyes almost as big as George's football. They did not dare to move, but at the same time felt embarrassed to be there. They held their breath to try to catch a little more of what was going on inside.

'Meghan, don't pull so fast. It's going to spill all over. Take a tissue and hold it over the top.'

'Haven't got one at hand. Oh, no, it's too late, it shot out already. Oh, dear, it's all over my dress.'

'Don't worry about your dress. We're lucky it's white. And we can easily clean the floor.'

There was the sound of water running and a brush being pushed over a surface.

'Let's do one more, Harry, OK?'

'Sure, go on.'

Another round of squeaking …

'Wait, Meghan, slow down.'

'Why? It's going so smoothly.'

'No, wait, damn, it's broken. You pulled too quickly

and now it's broken. It will take a while to get this sorted.'

William tried to keep a neutral expression on his worried face.

'I'm so sorry, Harry. I am not used to doing this so many times, one after another.'

'Don't worry; we will practise this a lot more going forward.'

Kate looked at William, bewildered, yet aroused, and said very dryly, 'I promise I won't break your valuables.'

The rushing noise of the two children running down the hallway distracted William and Kate's attention for a few seconds. But the kids were quicker, and George pushed the kitchen door open before his parents could hold him back.

Silence.

A red-cheeked Harry appeared, sweat on his face, his hands hidden behind the cooking island. In the background a confused Meghan seemed to be trying to clean something up.

William cleared his throat, trying to present the impression of only having accidentally walked by.

'What?' Harry asked.

'"What" what?' William stammered.

Harry moved from the cooking island, holding a bottle of white wine in one hand and a corkscrew with half of a broken cork in the other. 'Overscrewed,' he remarked, looking at William. 'Typical. Lack of practice.'

This didn't help William or Kate look any less flabbergasted.

A very embarrassed Meghan stepped out of the kitchen, some wet spots on her otherwise immaculate dress.

The Driving Lesson

It was time for Meghan to adapt to driving on the left-hand side, as well as to learn how to manually change gears. Every person spending time in the British countryside should know how to drive a good old Land Rover. Back in America she had learnt to drive on the right-hand side, and only with automatic vehicles.

To keep it undercover, Harry decided to do the training himself. He didn't want to raise more attention than necessary. Since Meghan had stepped into his life, they were always in the spotlight and under constant observation by the press. Although he had been used to it since childhood, Harry tried to avoid it as much as he could.

He decided to make his old army Jeep available for the training. The possible damage would not be a major loss. Although it was not too easy to steer, at least the gearbox was quite robust and willing to forgive many mistakes. For the terrain he chose the private grounds of Kensington Palace, well away from the public eye. A few short distances would be good enough for the first lesson.

It was a bright morning in early November, the advent season only a month away, anticipating the approach of Christmas, the air crisp and clear and full of promise. This was the perfect time, Harry thought, smiling to himself as he strolled over to the garage to take the little beast out of the cave.

Meghan was filled with excitement. She had loved Harry's car from the beginning, and, knowing that cars are boys' best friends, she felt honoured to be allowed to drive his darling. She felt that a shabby-chic combination would be perfect and dressed in a very sexy way, with provocative high heels, a very short mini displaying her freshly shaved endless legs, a blouse with a décolleté showing more than hiding and the makeup she had recently acquired at Selfridges. She left the car to play the shabby part in the combination.

To tease Harry even more she wore her hair loose and wild, feeling a bit like a cougar, with long nails and ready to attack. Harry would like this; she was sure of that. He always liked it when serious things were combined with a bit of erotica and exotica. On former occasions they had found that they had a mutual understanding on this.

Harry had already parked the Jeep outside; he didn't want to create an opportunity to have it ruined right at the beginning when driving out of the garage. The door to the driver's seat was open, conveying a warm welcome.

Harry was casually standing next to the door, anticipating nothing unusual, when the sight of Meghan approaching almost slammed him back into the car. Just like in a movie, in slow motion, Wonder Woman was approaching on Empire State Building-like high heels, the muscles of her perfectly shaped legs moving in harmony with every step she took. The wind played with her long, loose hair, her eyes darting into his, her breasts in perfect rhythm with her wagging hips.

Harry almost fainted. He soaked in every moment with accelerated heartbeat. With a dry swallow, he tried to stay grounded and concentrate on what was coming next, not

71

what was trying to get hold of him in his secret wishes.

When Meghan was close to Harry, she pressed her curvy body into his, feeling his muscles harden, and purred into his hairy ear, 'Hi, darling. Are you ready?'

'Oh, Meghan, I'm so ready! If only you knew ...'

'Yeah, I feel it right now ...' and with a meaningful glance, first down to the centre of his body and then back upward into his shining eyes, she laughed and tried to get into the car, tripping over his large feet in her endless high heels.

Headfirst, she landed in the car, making a big arc through the air. This was good for Harry, as he could get a glimpse under her short skirt at the colour and shape of her knickers. This turned him on even more.

By the time Harry had managed to run around the car to the passenger door, Meghan had been able to shift her position and get seated upright in front of the steering wheel. He was about to get into the car when Meghan made a fanning motion with her long nails, indicating that he should stay out.

'What?' Harry asked.

'Please stay out and watch while I turn the car,' Meghan said proudly. 'I have done some training with a friend back in Canada and am very capable of driving; I will show you!'

With a big frown on his forehead, Harry stepped back, not daring to complain, anxious not to destroy the promising rest of the day with sexy Meghan. Reluctantly, he positioned himself directly behind the left rear wheel, ready to give signs in case Meghan needed to know about something in her blind spot.

Harry started to perspire. Meghan showed him her best

thousand-gigawatt smile, lipstick everywhere in and outside her mouth, brimming with self-confidence.

She started the engine, and the motor howled like a horde of wolves. She must have pressed the accelerator a tick too firmly.

Harry hid his face in his hand. *This is already starting well,* he thought.

With major cracking sounds coming out of the gearbox, she finally managed to put the desired gear in and started letting the clutch go so slowly that it started to smoke, until with a sudden bang she let it go completely and the car took a jump backwards. She had seemingly missed the forward gear and got the rear gear instead.

This unforeseen movement was too quick for Harry to react. The car jumped directly over his wide and bulky shoes with the back wheel. With a cry louder than the sound of the engine, he reported his misery, but Meghan was too focused on her task to notice it over the engine noise.

She thought she had driven over a bump and managed to stop the car immediately with an abrupt pull of the handbrake. Outside the car she could make out a bent-down Harry. Frightened to death, she released the handbrake, mistook the accelerator for the brake and reared back further, hitting Harry's shoes again, this time with the front wheel. This made him sink to the ground entirely, sobbing on his back.

Finally, Meghan was able to bring the car to a complete stop by turning the engine off without pressing the clutch, causing the car to make another jump. Swallowing with a pale face, she sat in front of the steering wheel, trying to grasp what had happened, until Harry's ongoing screaming took her out of her thoughts. Hurriedly she rushed outside and helped Harry to get upright, trying to comfort him.

Luckily, Harry had instinctively put on his robust army boots, which had protected him from the worst. His toes were probably turning blue, but not broken.

It took Meghan a very long time to calm her wincing Harry and to persuade him to take a seat in the car.

Harry was highly suspicious. He kept his hand at the handbrake, ready to pull it up with all his force. He also left the window open, not telling Meghan that it was not so he could get some fresh air, but so he could maintain an emergency escape route. Nervously, he waited for whatever happened next.

But, before Meghan made any attempt to start the engine again, she announced with an air of great significance, putting her long-nailed forefinger up in the air, 'Wait, I forgot *one* important thing!'

With a sly smile she crawled out of the car, fumbling in her pocket. Harry got impatient inside. What was she doing? She could refresh her lipstick later; this was training time!

Outside, a sudden puffing sound could be heard and, before he could intervene, Meghan came back into the car, placing her half-inflated toilet seat on the driver's seat.

Harry's eyes were bigger than eggs. 'Honey, what's that now?'

'You told me to always use this toilet seat when I sit somewhere other than at home, and I am quite sure that it will help me with driving,' Meghan replied with her broadest smile, climbing into the car. 'I have a better view from up here.'

She was sitting very high with the toilet seat underneath her, her hair touching the ceiling. Harry rolled his eyes but let her do her thing. He knew he'd rather not tangle with a woman, and especially this one, once she had an opinion.

Ready for the next lesson, Meghan started the engine and smiled promisingly at the shivering Harry sitting next to her. 'Are you ready, darling?'

'Yeees,' Harry replied, intensifying his tight hold on the handle of the door. The little ginger hair left on his head stood out a tick more than normal.

Meghan surprisingly found first gear and then made the Jeep jump forward and stop a few times, not in complete control of the clutch. This was not too bad; in fact, it was just what Harry had expected. The continued jumping and stopping got into a rhythm and made Harry relax as it got smoother over time. It conveyed the feeling of being in a cradle, swinging back and forth, unconsciously bringing up his beloved childhood memories. He liked it; he felt safe.

His relaxation came to a halt when, with a tremendous sound, the engine howled up. She had let the clutch go and at the same time pressed the accelerator like a fool. The car sped up, completely out of control. Everything happened so quickly that Harry could not react by pulling the handbrake, both of them yelling together as the garage door approached too fast. By some miracle Meghan managed to pull the steering wheel around and with screeching tires the car missed the garage wall by millimetres, then whirled to the right, uprooting a barrowful of the garden flowers that were planted there.

Meghan was so scared as the plants rushed by her

window that she let the wheel go and lifted her hands up, holding her head, yelling as uncontrollably as the movement of the car. Harry pressed his back firmly into the seat while wildly pushing his feet to the floor as a reflex, not comprehending why his attempt to brake didn't work. They were changing direction depending on what obstacles the front wheels found on the ground. The car managed to pass through the open gates that led into the park and started to head towards the pond, across the freshly manicured lawn.

When Meghan glanced through two fingers, her hands still covering her face, and realising what was going on, she instinctively tried to get back control, her feet looking for the brake pedal. Adding to her misery, her high heels were stuck in the carpet. With a last desperate attempt to reach the brake, she made a big swing and pressed the only pedal she could find.

The Jeep's bonnet rose again like a horse speeding up, lifting the car for a short moment.

Harry's arms were whirling around, trying to get hold of anything that would give him security. He grabbed Meghan's seat adjustment lever and, without intending to, pulled it up sharply, allowing Meghan's seat to recline fully with one swift movement and lifting her yelling to another octave.

Of course, Meghan's feet were lifted up as well, not at all where they should be any more. Her high heels had drilled firmly into the carpet and brought the fabric up with them. This in turn made the carpet get stuck like a cake roulade on the accelerator. The pedal was now fixed at full throttle position.

Meghan was stretched to her full horizontal length,

which caused the toilet seat to jerk and move to the front as there was no weight on it any more. The inflated rubber seat became an unwelcome obstacle and hindered Meghan's efforts to get back to the driver's position. The car continued its uncontrolled race towards the duck pond.

Harry understood that the only thing that could rescue both of them was his personal intervention now. He therefore bent down and tried to crawl forward to get access to the pedals. His idea was to operate the brake pedal by hand, knowing that the handbrake would never be sufficient at this speed.

Unfortunately, the car hit some bushes and therefore started to swing around, driving in bends. This caused Harry to swing as well. Every time he was within reach of the pedals, the car made him lose control again and he was thrown back, unable to touch the brake pedal.

By this time, one of the gardeners had heard the commotion and become alarmed. He saw the car and knew that ahead of it lay the immense pond; it could only be a few more seconds before it splashed directly into the water. Horror was written on the gardener's face.

Meghan suddenly had a bright moment and gathered her thoughts. Lying stretched out, she had no chance to get back control of the car, but she had her hands free and therefore tried to grab the handle to open the door. Straining like it was her last chance, she got hold of the handle and pulled it. She was now able to free her right leg from the borehole in the carpet, and with her foot she gave the door a kick to make it spring open. But the door did not stay open and forcefully fell back towards her.

With her high heel, she had a good, long tool to stick

out with which she tried to stop the door from closing again. The door had such a weight and such an enormous swing that the high heel bored a hole through the metal sheet of the Jeep. Terrified, Meghan realised that she had now manoeuvred herself into an even worse position, stuck to the car and bound to its fate.

While Meghan was firmly drilled into the door and Harry was rolling on the floor, the car continued its approach to the pond. The gardener stood with his mouth wide open, unable to speak or make any sound, paralysed and watching in shock.

The car hit the rim of the fountain, which sloped gently upward. The angle was perfect for a long-haul trajectory.

As if in slow motion, the car was rising like a jet plane, the wheels turning in the air, the engine howling. It inclined more to the right, causing the door that Meghan was stuck in to open completely. The strap of her shoe broke; she fell, leaving her high heel behind, and Harry was shaken out into the air after her.

With cries in the air, longer and louder than anything the gardener had ever heard, the car finally reached its peak and started its descent. Just seconds after Meghan and Harry had hit the water, the car made a huge splash when it plunged into the pond, a safe distance from the lost passengers.

While the car was still visible on the surface, Meghan and Harry were not. Waves were splashing to the sides of the large pond. The gardener instinctively shut his mouth and swallowed.

Silence.

With a final roar from the exhaust, the car slowly sank into the pond, after the last ducks had made a hot start and were safely airbound. Only bubbles gave a hint to what had just happened.

Now, still in slow motion, the gardener realised that his head was shaking from left to right. He watched his own hair swing from one side to the other, while he heard his own voice crying, 'Noooooooooooo ...'

After what felt like an eternity, he saw first Meghan's and then Harry's head popping out of the water. This was the release the gardener needed to get out of his shock, finally feeling his body again. He pulled all his muscles together and sprinted to the pond.

Meghan was floating on some kind of odd, roundish rubber device and Harry was paddling like an old steamer, pulling her behind him. Harry would not have believed that the inflatable toilet seat could serve as a life raft too.

When they were within hearing distance, the gardener stopped and watched as Harry and Meghan approached the edge of the pond.

Harry looked up into the ash-pale face of the gardener and, after spitting out some water, he said with a very grumpy and hoarse voice, 'What? I just wanted to introduce Meghan to my private swimming pool.'

*

Meghan didn't like being exposed to ridicule and therefore decided to put things right after the driving lesson debacle with Harry. When students failed, it was usually the result of a bad teacher and not the student's incapability. The former training with her friend in Canada must have been unsuccessful. Or perhaps Harry's presence had put too much expectation and therefore pressure upon her. Or she had been given the wrong tool to properly demonstrate her skills. Surely the ex-army vehicle was totally useless. After all, the dated Jeep was no stylish car. No wonder things had gone wrong.

Meghan had told Harry the truth before their first lesson. She really did have driving experience and had done some training before. She just could not understand how things had got so completely out of hand, with the effect that she had been put into a most unfavourable light. She imagined there could have been a few other reasons for her failure: the car having the steering wheel on the wrong side, the car not being suitable for driving in high heels, the car having the pedals in the wrong place or perhaps the car having the order of the gears the wrong way round. One thing was clear, though: she was a good driver, and she would prove it to Harry. She was going to reset her own self-esteem and thereby change Harry's perception of her driving skills.

She took all her courage and decided to go for a drive on her own. She had contacted a good friend of hers, who had organised an old but reliable Ford Fiesta that Meghan was going to use for her self-training.

It was another chilly morning in November, and the sun was just about to rise when early bird Meghan stole herself out of the small and cosy Nottingham Cottage, with Harry fast asleep.

To get things one hundred percent right, Meghan decided to wear less lipstick and more suitable gear this time, for the cold weather and for the task ahead of her. This meant no high heels and no miniskirt, but indigenous wellies, thin leather gloves, a warm cashmere pullover and a warm cap over her head and ears. She had learned from her former mistakes. With this gear she felt much more English, and that would help her in her driving attempt.

The car stood in a private car park not far away from their cottage. The friend had told her that the car still needed a small service and number plates as it had been taken off the road more than a year ago. However, Meghan thought for this short trip it would be OK. The car would still run a few miles without having been serviced, and she could drive this short distance without number plates; she was a Hollywood star after all, and surely certain rules could be applied with some flexibility.

As she took her seat, she realised that the windscreen was covered with damp. She had to crawl out of the small car once again, taking her woollen scarf to wipe the fogged-up windows. The damp had partially frozen over the glass and it took her several minutes to de-ice. This action made her fingers stiff; as a native Californian girl she still could not adapt to the often unfriendly weather in England.

Back in the driver's seat, she sighed as she turned the key to engage the engine. The immediate purring sound made her feel at ease again; the engine seemed to obey her commands and do as she wished. Being of a cheerful nature, she whistled a melody as she started to manoeuvre the car out of the car park. After the usual beginner problems like letting go of the clutch inappropriately, stalling the engine and producing a hot start with a screech from the tires, she managed to stabilise herself in a more or less continuous driving mode. This helped her to settle down, allowing her perspiration to stop dripping underneath her thick woollen cap.

Finally, she made it; she was on her journey on open roads. She felt like an astronaut being shot into endless space, travelling alone in her cosy satellite. In a good mood, she dared to take a turn at the third junction, which led her out of the Kensington Palace area. It was early in the morning and therefore there wasn't much traffic. Meghan had a very good sense of direction and felt secure enough to drive off to other areas of the city. The further she drove, the more her self-confidence grew, and soon she felt bold enough to extend her ride further and further.

She had set her iPhone to play her favourite songs and left it on the passenger seat, filling the car with buzzing music. Singing loudly, clapping along whenever possible, she totally forgot about her surroundings. She had probably been driving for almost an hour when the sudden blare of a horn shook her out of her journey through the clouds.

Back on earth, she realised that traffic was starting to jam, with cars everywhere. She tried to change lanes, forgetting she was supposed to be driving on the left, until another car forced her to pay attention to her mistake. This sudden mistake put her completely back into her unease, making her feel overloaded. All her insecurity came back and caused her to make one mistake after the other.

It ended with Meghan being blocked in by several cars, in a wonderful chorus of horns, so nobody could move any more. It was so terrifying that she instinctively closed her eyes, put her hands over her ears to protect herself against the immense noise and started to scream helplessly. For something like a minute she continued this ritual, and when she reopened her eyes the other cars had disappeared.

Suddenly a very loud horn blared from behind her. This was her sign to leave the scene quickly and, in a firm attempt to flee, she pressed the accelerator with such power that the engine howled and catapulted her out of her misery.

Traffic lights flew by; some looked green and a few others looked rather red. People were waving and screaming as she rushed past them. It all felt like an accelerated dream. Again, Meghan closed her eyes and screamed out a high-pitched sound of despair, pressing the accelerator even harder while staying in second gear in order to escape from that nightmare. Shops and advertisements looked like a smeared stroke of paint as her car sped past them.

Horns and blinking and howling left and right, in front of and behind her, she suddenly saw what looked like a country road off the main street. This seemed like a door to heaven. Courageously she turned the car in a sharp ninety-degree angle, almost frontally hitting an oncoming car, and took the less busy road, not realising that she had been washed into Hyde Park.

It was like she had entered paradise. Suddenly the traffic was gone. Meghan found herself in the midst of beautiful nature, a park with mature trees and ponds. She was so glad to have escaped that urban horror, thinking she must be out of London, somewhere in the countryside or the suburbs. Happily, she blew the suppressed air out of her lungs, breathing in fresh air with a long sigh of relief. She was so glad she was still alive and that she had instinctively taken the way to better fields.

After driving like this for a couple of half-conscious minutes, she saw a branch off onto a muddy path. *How nice,* she thought. This would surely lead her to further remoteness.

Happily, she swung the car over and slowed down, as the dirt and small stones made a thundering noise below her. Back at ease, she started to drift off into her thoughts again, until a movement on the right made her jump in her seat. What was that? Had she really just seen a horse overtake her? And on the right side? (She had forgotten that overtaking was done on the right-hand side in England.) She clearly recalled having seen the bewildered face of the rider who had passed her.

Furious, she tried to grab the window handle on the right-hand door to open it, which nearly caused her to drive off into a bush. Somehow, she managed to pull the car back to the muddy road at the last second and bring it to a stop. The rider had slowed down his horse and was waiting alongside the path.

She opened her window and yelled out, 'What? Are you crazy or what, riding a horse on a normal road like that?'

Hoarse from screaming so loudly in the early morning, she shook her head. Crazy Englishmen; she just could not understand these folks. They should ride on bridle paths and not on open roads.

The crazy Englishman in return shook his head more violently than Meghan, then straightened his back and put the horse back on the road without saying a word, galloping away.

After a few minutes, Meghan had calmed down enough to proceed on her journey. The road became more and more rural, with a few small hillocks causing the soft fabric of her cap to touch the ceiling of the car with each unexpected bump. This reminded her of life itself with its ups and downs, and her own wise analogy made her smile proudly. She was infinitely full of herself.

The car almost stalled again, as it slowed down too much with Meghan not changing gears accordingly. After another bump, an almost invisible sandy area appeared so quickly that Meghan was unprepared to swing the car around and bring it to safe terrain.

There she was, stuck in the sandy, muddy ground. No reversing, no pulling forward could take her out of her misery. After a few wheel-spinning manoeuvres, only making her sink deeper into the sand and mud, she finally gave up, turning off the engine.

After a prolonged sigh, a loud knock on the window made her jump again, higher than from the previous bumps in the road. Her head painfully hit the ceiling of the car. Looking outside, she saw someone grinning in at her. Blinking her eyes with their long fake lashes a few times, she managed to make out a male face, looking exactly like the horse rider she had seen before.

As Meghan opened the window, the rider greeted her in a friendly way, asking her whether she needed help. She did, she explained, displaying her Hollywood-white but yet unbrushed teeth. She felt she had made the best possible impression on the gallant stranger, who was fumbling around in his dated tweed jacket.

'Would you like to take a sip of my whisky? It helps calm you down in unforeseen situations,' the rider offered, grinning like a horse with his big yellow teeth.

Not sure whether she should try to escape or grab the bottle, she decided to do the latter, as she was really at a loss and the rider really seemed to want to help. Swallowing the liquid immediately gave her a warm feeling and sudden comfort. She decided to take another slurp, but this time a bigger one. The rider smiled again, insisting she keep the bottle and offering to arrange help as quickly as he could.

What Meghan did not understand was that the English gentleman totally disagreed with her rude and unacceptable behaviour, and was not amused at all by her driving on bridle paths in the middle of Hyde Park. Keeping his countenance, he appeared so friendly that any English person would have understood how furious he in fact was.

Feeling the whisky streaming through her veins, Meghan settled down completely, knowing that rescue was not far. Preparing for having to wait a certain amount of time until the promised help was here, she closed the window to keep a bit of the heated air in the car and pulled the cap further down over her face, stowing her long hair well underneath it in order to help keep in the warmth. She took another slurp and another one, self-pity grabbing her in an unwelcome way. How could she have put herself in such a miserable position again? But then, rescue was coming and she would soon be helped.

She hadn't eaten before her venture, and, as her eyes drooped, her mind started to swim with far too much alcohol in an empty stomach. The whisky did its job efficiently and put her to sleep very quickly, exhausted from all the road challenges.

A sudden knock on the window made Meghan flail with her hands and feet at once. It was so uncontrolled that she pressed the horn in her shock, which made her jump even more in the seat. Horrified, she tried to lift her arms for help, but her hands hit the low ceiling and she finally realised where she was. Her mind quickly brought her back to her merciless reality.

Another knock from the two policemen made her open the window.

'Can I see your driving licence, please, sir?' one of the policemen asked, taking Meghan for a lad, as she looked like a young man with her cap pulled over her face and no makeup at all.

'What? I don't need a driving licencccccce,' Meghan babbled, a treacherous smell coming out of her mouth.

The policeman made a wry face, realising from the way she spoke and smelled that she must have been drinking. 'Get out of the car, lad,' he said in a more unfriendly and commanding way. 'And where are your number plates?'

'I don't neeesh number platesh either,' Meghan firmly responded.

'OK, boy, enough. Where do you live? What is your address?' shouted the policeman.

'My adressh ish Kenshington Palash, Harry can tell you the detailsh,' Meghan answered, gesticulating wildly.

'Stop this now and get out of the car immediately,' commanded the police officer.

'What car?' Meghan yelled, chortling.

The face of the policeman started to get pinkish. 'Get the hell out of the car now!' he screamed back at Meghan.

'Wow, thish wash loud,' she replied, blinking her eyes innocently with astonishment.

'This is not a dishwasher; it is a car,' the second officer called at her, giving his colleague a bold smile.

As Meghan showed no signs of intending to open the door, the first policeman started to hammer on the roof of the car.

Meghan giggled. 'What? Want to come inshide?'

By now the policeman's face was a nice warm scarlet. 'Get out of the car now; you are arrested!' he stated with vehemence. 'The charges against you are, among others: drunk driving, driving without a driving licence, driving without number plates, potential theft of a car, potentially carrying a false identity, failure to obey police orders and insulting police officers.'

Meghan's forefinger wagged. 'No, no, dear man, I shan't go to prishon – nor to rehab for shat matter. D'you know who I am?'

The policeman was turning a dangerous shade of blue.

'I am M ... eghan Marrrkle. Maaarkle like Shbaaaaarkle,' she added, prolonging *sparkle* while poking her tongue out. Meghan was almost not able to articulate, so furious was she.

The policeman could hardly contain himself any more. Was this rascal trying to kid him? 'So you are Eggham Sharkle?! And I am the Queen.' With a swift movement, he managed to sneak his arm through the open window and pull the lock button to unlock the car.

'I don't shink the Queen will be amushed to learn that you have arreshted me for no reashon atshall,' Meghan shouted, this long and most challenging sentence followed by an uncontrolled loud fart escaping her body.

'To keep things straight,' the policeman replied, 'the Queen has vested in me the right to arrest people who commit traffic offences.'

While Meghan was still processing the words the policeman had just said, the door of the car was flung open and Meghan torn out of it quicker than she would ever have been able to leave on her own.

'Oh, thash wash fast,' Meghan sang out loud, suddenly brimming with joy.

'You are now being brought to the detoxication department of the local police station, where you will have to stay until you are sober again and we have checked your identity,' the policeman stated with great importance.

After an uncontrolled, very unladylike burp into the policeman's face, Meghan waved her hand loosely, pronouncing, 'At leasht I have my toilet sheat with me, alwaysh prepared ...' and leaving the policeman with even bigger question marks than before.

The Riding Out

Christmas was approaching fast; preparations were already in full swing, and a formal family gathering at Sandringham House was only a few weeks away. It was time for Meghan to take a ride. Not a ride in a car, but a real horseback ride.

Harry was a passionate polo rider; he and his brother made a dream team. Camilla had been an excellent participant in the ride to hounds. And everybody knew how much horses meant to the Queen and how fond she was of the noble creatures. Besides her corgis she loved horses above all else, being a passionate rider herself and a keen horse breeder. If Meghan truly wanted to make her place in the royal family, she needed to prove that she looked good when in the saddle.

Having been riding in the Grand Canyon and elsewhere on several occasions, Meghan was confident enough to agree to Harry's suggestion that she have a ride out with Camilla. He had organised everything for a fabulous afternoon at Sandringham estate, where they would have gorgeous countryside and could ride for miles, well away from the public eye. Meghan liked Camilla a lot. A relaxed girls' chat on horseback while striding through English nature would be a welcome distraction from serious royal everyday life.

To make a proper first impression – one never has a

second chance to make a first impression – Meghan had gone to a professional riding store to purchase an exclusive hunting outfit. At home, she had always been riding in the relaxed Western style, but of course she had investigated and knew exactly how a traditional, formal hunting outfit would look.

It was a bright morning and Meghan was standing there at the stables, brimming with joy. She had opted for an elegant blue coat, white trousers as the rule required, black leather riding boots, leather gloves, a helmet and, of course, a crop.

When Camilla spotted her waiting there, she said, 'Oh, you want to go riding in hunting style. I thought you'd rather just have a stroll through the park, but in that case I shall quickly change my attire to match yours. I'll be back in a few minutes,' and off she went, leaving Meghan a little bit doubtful.

After Camilla had changed, Meghan approached the horse from the right-hand side and made an effort to mount it. Camilla let out a high-pitched cry, and, uttering a hoarse laugh, she said, 'Oh, Meghan, I like that. You've already made the first mistake. This will cost you a drink when we stop at the pub!'

Meghan's eyes widened. What had she done wrong? She had not done anything at all.

The head groom, who had been listening to the conversation, quickly ran over to Meghan and made her understand behind his hand: 'You should never ever mount a horse from anywhere other than the left-hand side. Horses are trained like that. Mounting a horse from the wrong side is a crime among riders and it will cost you a penalty – usually a drink for your fellow riders!'

Meghan's knees started to weaken. She had very much expected a better start than this.

The groom guided the insecure Meghan around the horse to the other side. Camilla was already sitting firmly in the saddle, looking down in amusement at what was going on. After a few awkward attempts, the head groom had to help Meghan mount by making his hands into a foothold and lifting her up.

Almost up, Meghan was desperately looking for the big saddle horn she was used to on the huge Western saddles. Not finding any hold, she almost dropped down on the other side of the saddle, but fortunately the stable master managed to get hold of her leg and with joy provided support to a part of her bottom in the last second to keep her up.

With a lot of effort, she finally sat in the saddle, feeling most uncomfortable. This was so strange. The saddle was tiny and slippery, not like the comfy and huge frying-pan-like saddle she was used to in Western style. And then the stirrups! How was she supposed to stay in these delicate things? She was used to large openings that she could put her boot in, made of leather. This saddle had stirrups made of metal, which made it so much more difficult to stay in place. And then what about the reins? Here in England they seemed to be much shorter and bound together. Western style had long and loose reins; one could grab them in any way one liked.

By now, Meghan was utterly uncomfortable and, as her doubts were rising, she was tempted to mention them carefully to Camilla. She also hoped to pick up a few tricks while watching how Camilla managed her horse. But when she turned, Camilla was already moving away on her horse.

Meghan looked down at the stable master with question marks in her eyes. He quickly gave her a few rudimentary instructions, finally slapping the horse tenderly on the back to make it go, and she was off on her riding adventure.

She was almost not capable of keeping up with Camilla. She tried to make her horse accelerate, but somehow the animal ignored her totally. The horse walked from the right border to the left and back again, stopping wherever the best grass was growing. A nightmare for Meghan! With some heavy kicking of her legs, she finally managed to slowly advance the horse.

Camilla was in an excellent mood and seemed entirely at ease in her saddle. One could tell it was home territory for her. This didn't give Meghan any relief; it made it rather worse.

After a few minutes of not talking at all, with Meghan breathing heavily from the physical effort, completely absorbed by trying to handle her horse, Camilla said, 'They are warm enough now; let's trot!'

And before Meghan could open her mouth, Camilla was trotting away. Meghan's horse wanted to keep up with its friend and started to trot itself, making her even more insecure. The remnants of her riding knowledge told her that one should always tell the horse what to do and not let it take over control. Gasping for air, Meghan tried to keep up.

Riding behind Camilla, Meghan tried to copy her movements: up and down, up and down, up and down. Inside Meghan's head, her brain started to bang around;

she was not used to this. In Western riding one kept sitting in the 'frying pan', legs stretched and relaxed, very easygoing. This stuff here was so strenuous; it was almost impossible to find the right rhythm with the horse. Even after a short while, Meghan was exhausted. Where would this lead?

Meghan tried to change her riding mode by keeping herself seated firmly in the saddle, but it banged her around even harder. She felt like a jackhammer, torturing her own and the horse's back. With every bump her confidence started to sink. Every hit knocked her down more.

Luckily, Camilla gave a sign to slow down and they got back to walking again. Time for Meghan to relax. But now Camilla was speaking like a never-ending cascade of waterfalls. Being polite, Meghan had to follow her speech very attentively and make a remark from time to time rather than focusing her mind on the horse and trying to figure out how to control it.

When they came around a few bushes, a wide field suddenly opened up in front of them. The horses felt the width and with it the freedom, instinctively wanting to set off galloping. They started to get nervous, dancing around and waiting for the final command to gallop.

Meghan was horrified and turned to Camilla, trying to warn her that a gallop might not be the best idea. Camilla was gone already. Meghan's cry was drowned by the dashing sound of the galloping horseshoes as her mount took off after Camilla's, and the one thing that kept her in the saddle was her instinct to grab the horse's mane.

Trying to keep up with Camilla's horse, Meghan's horse sped up; it was anxious not to stay behind. Meghan was trying to hold it back, but the horse became more and more furious. Finally, when it couldn't bear Meghan's pulling on its reins and mane any more, it took a sudden jump and kicked its back legs in the air, trying to get rid of its highly unpleasant baggage.

Meghan's cry was absorbed in her throat and never became audible, so unprepared was she for this change of course. Somehow, she managed to stay in the saddle, but in the chaos she lost her crop. Her horse reached such a speed that eye water was running like tears over Meghan's pale cheeks and the wind was blowing in her ears. It felt faster and more furious than anything she had experienced in her life before.

Breathing heavily, she finally caught up with Camilla, who had changed to walking again. Meghan's horse almost bumped into the back of Camilla's horse, so fast was her uncontrolled approach.

Smiling brightly, Camilla said, 'Well, that was a nice, soft warm-up. On the next field we should allow the horses to heat it up a bit more.'

This time Meghan protested loudly, making her misery clear to Camilla. Camilla was not very receptive to Meghan's wretchedness. She only responded without batting an eyelash, 'I see you lost your crop; that will cost you a double drink. Ha ha!'

This was a great opportunity to stop this crazy Englishwoman, and Meghan blurted out in despair, 'Yes, let's go to the next pub, I am so thirsty!' She absolutely needed a rest and she felt her bottom was probably bleeding by now.

Looking down at her legs, Meghan realised in horror that they trembled like aspen leaves. She was still feeling the aftershocks of the previous gallop. Camilla noticed her glancing down and flicked her eyes in the same embarrassing direction. This made Meghan hurriedly widen the corners of her mouth, a broad slit appearing over her whole face, almost touching each ear. Meghan displayed the most unnatural and artificial smile Camilla had seen in her entire life.

With a cracked voice Meghan squeaked, 'I'm not only thirsty, but also cold. Let's have a hot shot of double vodka martini!'

Camilla burst out laughing. She liked that. Raw and direct.

Arriving at the pub, Meghan did not know how to get off the horse. With the greatest awkwardness any observer had ever seen, she finally managed to touch ground again, almost crying from relief when she felt the earth underneath her. But the relief didn't last long. As soon as she was standing, the effects of the ride hit her; all her muscles were sore and she could hardly walk.

Camilla was laughing loudly. She had naturally observed Meghan's pain, but she said, 'Meghan, you will get used to it sooner or later, don't worry; you'll have to get used to many things in this country,' which made Meghan even feel worse.

One thing Meghan was more than convinced of was that she would never, ever agree to horse riding again.

After two stiff drinks, the world started to turn around Meghan. She needed that like a bullet in the head: a dizzy mind for the upcoming exertion.

Camilla somehow seemed fitter than before. With an elegant swing she mounted the horse again, waiting for poor Meghan. By this time, Meghan was so worn down she could not imagine she had any capacity for embarrassment left and frankly did not care. Therefore, she announced to Camilla that she needed to go to the ladies' first.

After a very long time, Meghan came back. She had been thinking about escaping through the back window of the pub, but in the end hadn't, having weighed up the potential consequences.

Camilla had started to tap her foot in the stirrup, holding Meghan's horse. As Meghan came closer, Camilla's eyes narrowed. What was going on? Had Meghan put on some weight in her absence? Wouldn't it be more likely that she had lost weight after voiding her bowels? Or was her behind swollen somehow? As Meghan approached, it became clear that something was stuffed into the back of her trousers.

Meghan took the last of her dignity and stood on a nearby stone in order to get mounted. Her behind looked like a balloon.

'What's that up your trousers, Meghan?' Camilla asked in disgust.

Meghan put her shoulders back. Chin up, she sat upright in the saddle and replied in a typical upper-class tone, 'Always prepared with the toilet seat when life is at risk,' making Camilla burst out in laughter until she got hoarse.

*

The return trip turned out to be even more disastrous than the first leg. With her inflated toilet seat in her trousers, it was surely more comfortable for Meghan to sit in the saddle, but on the other hand she had less of a sense of where the saddle was. Once, she almost sat down beside the horse when the horse's back moved under her in an unexpected direction. In the last second, she managed to get hold of the mane again to protect her from the worst.

Camilla had the time of her life; never had she had such a joyful and funny ride out. She liked Meghan enormously and she was sure that this would not be their last time together on horseback.

Meghan felt dizzy and miserable, both sore and sick from being shaken like one of her vodka martinis. After Camilla insisted on stopping by another pub on the way, Meghan felt worse than terrible, whereas Camilla seemed to be in better shape than ever. Meghan was only hoping that they would reach the stables soon and this nightmare would come to an end.

They were walking along a dirt road, Meghan sitting dully in the saddle, her eyes half-closed, hardly able to recognise what was going on around her, when suddenly a car overtook them. Kicking up some dust, it made the two riders breathe quite a bit of it.

Meghan was at the end of her strength, but the reckless and rude behaviour of the car driver brought some of it back to her. She was filled with anger. Through the dust she was able to get a quick peek at the car. It looked like a green Land Rover, but she could not make out any number plate.

Perfect, she thought: *being a reckless driver and driving illegally without a number plate. Like attracts like!*

Meghan was furious; if only she had the chance to confront this person. She would tell the driver off at once, directly to their face.

But Camilla didn't seem upset at all, and Meghan was

so tired that it was too much effort for her to raise her voice. She resigned herself to the slow motion of the horse, only hoping she would be back home soon.

They continued their walk on the dusty road. After a few minutes they could see a car parked on the edge of the road in the far distance. As they approached, Meghan was able to recognise it as the very same car that had overtaken them. And indeed, getting closer, she saw that the car lacked a number plate. What nerve!

The bonnet was open and a person was leaning over it, looking at the engine, obviously trying to fix something. Gloatingly, Meghan thought this served them right; that was what they got for their behaviour.

With the horses drawing closer, she noticed to her astonishment that the driver appeared to be an elderly woman, wearing a headscarf. Well, that didn't make it better. On the contrary, Meghan thought that it was even more inappropriate for a woman to behave in such a way.

Meghan looked over at Camilla, sand crunching between her teeth. 'I wouldn't be surprised if this old bag didn't have a valid driving licence either.'

Camilla's face flushed and she tried to say something, but Meghan interrupted her to continue her rant.

'And look at the condition of the car. It must be at least forty years old and looks like it has not been serviced for years. No wonder it has finally broken down. Such cars should not be allowed on public roads.'

The old driver did not seem overly impressed by Meghan's comments and calmly carried on with her job under the bonnet. Both horses now stood side by side in front of the Land Rover, like gangsters facing the local sheriff in a miserable version of a Western movie.

In a desperate effort to make the driver speak, Meghan shouted at her, 'Don't you think you should stop driving a car and leave the repair of this rusty thing to someone who understands what it takes to be a mechanic?'

These words finally triggered a response from underneath the bonnet. 'My dear, I have been a car mechanic myself since as early as the Second World War, and I know only too well how to repair a Land Rover. In fact, I am almost done. This car is in perfect driving condition. It is a sturdy British car, after all, even if your own lack of mechanical skill does not allow you to understand this entirely.'

This well-worded and carefully conveyed response made Meghan soften her tone a bit. 'Well, fair point, well made,' she said, adding *old granny* in her mind. 'But that still does not allow you to drive around without number plates.' In her mind she saw victory. *Yes, eat this, old frump!* she thought to herself.

The old woman partially appeared from the bonnet, lifting herself up in a slow movement that did not appear completely painless. 'No, my dear Ms Markle. That in itself indeed does not.'

By now beads of perspiration had started to appear on Meghan's forehead. In her mind the dramatic tune 'Once Upon a Time' started to play. From where, for heaven's sake, did the old lady know her name? And didn't the voice sound familiar? Her brain was working at full speed. Meghan instinctively knew that something had to be very, very wrong.

The ongoing silence made the tension almost unbearable. A passing breeze which lifted a swirl of dust enhanced the surreal impression of a classic Western movie.

After a long pause, the elderly woman continued speaking. 'But you may have heard that there is someone in this country who does not need number plates, nor a driving licence for that matter. And that person is the Queen. And that is precisely who I happen to be,' she said, moving her headscarf to the side.

Camilla frowned seriously, biting her dry lips. They hung down on one side and provided such an opening that she easily could have stuck two, if not three cigarettes in it at once. She definitely looked better than Clint Eastwood in his best Western movies. Her muscles were tense, eyes narrowed to slits, her face showing a tortured expression. She felt almost as uncomfortable as Meghan, although she was not directly to blame. She had recognised the Queen's Land Rover immediately and felt a sense of responsibility for not having informed Meghan earlier.

For another unbearably long moment, the Queen's eyes were fixed on Meghan and Camilla. Nobody said a word. Sweat was dripping down both riders' backs. The Queen tightened her lips, still looking pitilessly at them.

It was then that an uncontrolled squeaking came out of Meghan's mouth; it sounded like a pig. The horses, frightened by the sudden noise, shied. And, just in time to help release the tension, a very loud triple-blow fart, like shots from a cannon, escaped from one of the horses. This made the stressful situation evaporate into thin air at once, and all three women burst out laughing.

'Oh, by the way, Meghan, is the tool you are using on your saddle part of some sort of new riding technique?' the Queen asked sternly. 'I haven't seen it before. What is it? Should I be informed about some new invention?'

Meghan's face was not red; it was luminous, like a harbour signal warning of an approaching storm. She was unable to invent a lie.

'I installed my inflatable toilet seat to ease the pain ...' Meghan replied, almost whispering, not daring to speak loudly.

'Oh, that's news. I am mildly amused,' the Queen replied very dryly, without giving away any expression on her frozen face.

Riding home, there was no conversation between Camilla and Meghan. Meghan tried to stay in the saddle, her embarrassment almost dragging her behind the horse.

The Bootcamp

To further boost their relationship, Harry decided to go camping with Meghan. It was a common test of his, and all his girlfriends so far had had to complete this procedure to make sure they would fit. With Meghan it should be no different.

Harry decided to go to the English countryside, along with a tent, outdoor stuff, cooking devices and sleeping bags. For his amusement, he also took Prince George's fake little pop gun with him. He managed to persuade the small boy to lend him the toy, promising to bring it back soon together with an even better one. His experience had shown that producing such a device would give real insight into a woman's character. Thus far, only once had the situation almost got out of hand, as the girl had become hysterical, but luckily he had got everything back under control in the end. In his camping tests, he would also introduce a few other things that might provoke fear: putting a spider in their tent, for example, or pretending he had seen a snake.

As a royal, one could easily get into serious trouble or tricky situations. It was important, therefore, to see whether the woman at his side would instinctively react correctly. Of course, she would receive training on other occasions, but nevertheless Harry was no man for a cowardly woman. He liked to protect, but when nervousness turned to terror it was over. After all, Harry was an experienced soldier who had been at war in Afghanistan and other dangerous places. He knew how to deal with critical situations. And he liked the kick. A bit of adrenaline kept one young and agile.

Little did Harry know about Meghan's intentions when he asked her to come camping. She immediately seemed excited about this romantic idea, but she had her own plans for him. After all, it was her chance to take revenge for the Slugsgate in the garden a while back.

And so they set off towards the M25, heading north and out of London. Harry's new old army Jeep, a replacement for the sunken one, was packed to bursting, and both Meghan and Harry full of anticipation for the upcoming adventure.

Unfortunately for Meghan, or luckily for Harry, it had just started drizzling when they arrived at a remote place in the countryside, only some woods to be seen and the sound of grazing sheep audible. Harry was thrilled; the surroundings made him feel at home.

'Oh, darling, why don't you start putting up the tent?' Harry suggested. 'I have to secure the car and hurry to get some dry wood for the fire.'

And with these words he left Meghan standing there, several bundles of army tent material lying at her feet. Meghan looked down, a few question marks rising in her head. Well, she had thought this would go a bit differently, but down she bent to take the first heavy item. She looked for a convenient place to install it.

When Harry came back after some twenty minutes, he was pleasantly surprised by Meghan's good decision on where to place their camp and by how far she had already got with it. A bit awkwardly, she stood in the centre of the tent and tried to erect the middle pole, but Harry quickly gave her a hand, and after only a few more minutes the tent was ready.

Harry was impressed. The former girlfriends had been much slower and had made mistakes at the beginning. So far, Meghan was outstanding! His heartbeat quickened as he visualised the two of them lying close to each other in the tent later on. The odour of the old army tent made him even more excited. This was the smell of true adventure.

Before going to look for the knife he pretended he had left in the car, he instructed Meghan to make a fire. Obviously, he took a while before he returned, buying himself more time by shouting from afar, 'Honey, I have to drive to a petrol station; I forgot to bring the knife, and we will definitely need one!'

Not surprisingly, Meghan also passed the fire test, and by his return a sizeable fire was crackling. Harry was so proud of his future wife; it could not have been better with her.

It was time to play the first joker. Harry went into the tent, opened his secret can and let out a huge but harmless spider, letting it crawl over Meghan's sleeping bag. He quickly got out of the tent again, allowing the spider to take its own course. Harry smiled. He expected Meghan to jump in the air and cry for help as soon as she saw the little beast. To make it meaner, he walked over to the fire and suggested to Meghan it was time to bring the food out. He had deliberately placed it in the back of the tent.

Having to go into the tent on her own was most welcome for Meghan, as she was quite ready to play her own joker now. Looking back over her shoulder, she reassured herself that Harry was out of hearing distance.

She grabbed her rucksack and quickly took out a glass full of slugs. Grinning, she looked at all the slimy tracks. The glass was almost opaque by now, so thick was the slime. In a quick movement, she opened the glass, put on some plastic gloves she had brought with her and placed the slugs carefully in a very cosy place. She was sure they would like it there.

Harry was fumbling around in the fire with a stick, pretending to shift the logs. He pricked his ears, but nothing could be heard from the tent. He got suspicious and walked closer.

In that moment Meghan came out with the required bag and, as she passed him, she said as if as an afterthought, 'Oh, by the way, there was a fat, hairy spider marching around on my sleeping bag. I let it free outside, just to let you know that you don't have to be afraid of it any more.'

With open mouth Harry stood there like a rock; he could not believe what he had just heard.

And so the evening took its course, with Meghan and Harry ending the dinner satisfied and full after enjoying the truly delicious grilled food, cuddled up in front of the warm fire, gazing into the soft colours of the embers. The wine did the rest to put both of them into a relaxed and happy mood. Harry was over the moon; Meghan had passed the tests in every respect. Only the pop gun remained as the last tricky hurdle.

As the heat from the remaining fire was quickly dwindling and a fresh breeze came up, it was time to sneak into the tent.

Harry was lying in his sleeping bag, on the verge of sleep, when he suddenly felt a soft touch on his toe. In order to avoid claustrophobia, he usually left the zip of his sleeping bag open. It was pitch dark, with no way to make out anything other than the deep black night. No question, Harry quickly got turned on.

'Oh, Meghan, how I like your soft skin,' he murmured, thinking it especially erotic that she had started at his feet.

She didn't reply, and Harry was sure she would rather touch than talk. The wind made the leaves rustle in the trees and Harry's words went unheard.

Suddenly, he had another soft kick: a very tender, but somehow wet touch wandering up his hairy back. Harry was thrilled; was this Meghan licking his shoulders?

'Ah, Meghie, sweetheart, you turn me on so much ...' An emotional groaning left his trembling beard.

With another strike, Harry stiffened and was almost catapulted onto his feet. There it was, directly touching him on his upper leg, wandering up towards the top of his legs and the beginning of his torso ... to the sweet spot. Harry's eyes started to roll back. Not in his keenest dreams would he have dared to imagine such a romantic night in the wilderness. The touch intensified and, almost itching, he started to giggle. 'Oh, Meghan, this is wonderful.'

But somehow Harry was touched and licked everywhere on his body. In the middle of his ecstasy, he managed to have one bright moment when suddenly the realisation struck him with immense power that he could not be touched by Meghan on all these spots at the same time. Horror started to creep up his body. With an almost suffocating voice, not wanting to confront the reality, he hoarsely stammered, 'M-Meghan ...?'

On the other side of the tent, Meghan had been woken by Harry's turning and moving in his sleeping bag, and finally, having heard her name, she sleepily answered, 'What is it ...?'

A repressed cry came out of Harry's beard, as at last he fully realised that no single touch was from Meghan. Trembling with great anxiety, he managed to let his hand wander towards one touch point, pressing his eyes shut, hoping that somehow that would help avoid the worst. His hand travelled down, and further down, until it touched a slimy track and he directly hit the soft body of a very moist slug.

With a heartbreaking yell, Harry felt a shockwave like lightning through his bones, first stretching his body to its longest possible extent and then bending it, cramp-like contractions hitting him uncontrollably.

Meghan was so drowsy she didn't quite get what was going on when suddenly Harry got to his feet. Trying to jump out of the narrow, twisted sleeping bag, he fell over in it and directly hit the centre pole of the tent. What didn't add to the stability of the tent was the fact that Meghan had not tied the poles together properly, and that was when the whole tent collapsed with a sudden crash.

Outside, the wind added to the confusion. Some rustling was heard here and there, then gone again, just to rise up from a different direction. It sounded as if a person or two were sneaking around the tent.

Meghan screamed, not realising what was going on. Harry, thinking that they would be attacked from outside, cried, 'We are under attack!' as he hopelessly tried to find his torch in the layers of fabric. Meghan was on all fours, turning around in circles, and could not find the exit to the tent.

The yelling from both of them had risen to a dangerous

level by the time Harry's fingers brushed against something that felt like iron. He assumed it was the pop gun, with which he at least could fire a warning shot. With great effort, he made another push in that direction, and suddenly he heard a snap. A great pain was travelling through his finger and arm, the like of which he had never experienced before in his life. Instinctively he pulled the arm back. Together with it came the mousetrap Meghan had installed before because she was terrified of mice. No animal in this world could shock her, except mice. No snake, no spider, no bear, no cougar.

Like a madman, Harry swung around on his feet, turning in circles, yelling and sobbing at the same time, letting out sounds that were not Harry-like. He sounded like another person completely. The thick fabric the tent was made of didn't help and rather altered Harry's cries into suffocated, strange noises.

Meghan somehow managed to get out of the tent, thinking that Harry had escaped, and mistook the person yelling in the tent for the villain. Hurriedly, she ran to the half-extinct fire, blinded by horror, trying to find some of the stacked logs that were left. She grabbed one, approached the moving tent with the yelling thing inside, raised the wood and brought it down with all her force onto the point where the yelling was loudest, where she assumed the head was.

Immediately, the screaming stopped and the thing sank to the ground, giving no sound other than severe groaning.

At the same time, Meghan galloped into the woods searching for Harry, completely out of her mind. After a few minutes, she lowered her hoarse voice, realising that something was wrong, and returned to the campsite. And only then was she able to hear a pained but familiar voice coming from under the tent where she had hit the supposed villain.

Her head started to swim and she was hardly able to hold herself upright on her shaking legs. 'Harry, is that you?' she asked with her last shred of strength, tears running down her pale cheeks.

Out of the miserable pile of demolished tent came something like 'Oh, Meghan,' Harry's crying swallowing the rest of the phrase.

The Kidnap Training

After the camping disaster, Harry decided that Meghan definitely needed some expert training in how to behave correctly in a serious situation. For a couple of weeks, he had a painful bump exactly where the bald part of his head was. Besides being uncomfortable, it was also embarrassing. Whenever possible, he put a cap on to hide it from curious looks. Of course, he did not let anybody know what had happened in order to protect himself and Meghan from ridicule, but he had to learn from the experience. He therefore opted for kidnap training.

As a former soldier and a now full-time royal, Harry was very accustomed to kidnapping procedures and felt prepared enough to carry out the training himself. Every royal had to undergo such training, and therefore it was more than natural that it was now Meghan's turn to do so.

To make it a bit more playful, he suggested to Meghan that they combine this with a tiny bit of sexiness, as both of them were always eager to try out something new. Naturally, Meghan was all for it, heart and soul, and therefore Harry instructed her to dress only in sexy underwear. He would take care of the rest. In fact, if she were kidnapped at home, the most likely attire in which a kidnapper would meet Meghan was sexy underwear.

Meghan had purposely gone shopping for this special occasion and, having spent two hours at Agent

Provocateur, she had found what she had in mind. She proudly swung her shopping bag when entering Nottingham Cottage.

Meghan prepared herself upstairs in the bathroom, and by the designated time she was lying on the bed, dressed only in a very provocative bra, panties, sexy suspender stockings and, to top it off, her still-shiny black wellies. She thought the boots would give things a little more kick, remembering their relatively early encounter when she had worn them in bed. She just wanted to give Harry an extra boost.

To make it a bit more mysterious, she had shut the blinds and put the bedroom into a shimmery twilight. It was almost dark, and Harry would not able to detect everything right away. This intensified all of it. She had also sprayed her favourite perfume in the room while her iPhone played some romantic tunes she had only downloaded recently.

Like this, fully prepared for the kidnap training, she was eagerly anticipating the upcoming episode.

Having lain there for a few minutes, she heard the doors being shut and locked downstairs. Harry seemed to be in an equally good mood to hers, humming a melody. Slowly, the humming came closer and she could hear Harry taking the steps upstairs. Her heartbeat quickened; she licked her lips, imagining the best of her wildest dreams.

Harry himself was very excited too. He had done some serious shopping from an erotic online shop to prepare for this event. When the parcel had arrived a few days ago, he had quickly stowed it in the garden shed under some old tools. The night before, when Meghan had been fast asleep, he had sneaked out with a torch to examine the contents and, to his delight, everything had been as he expected.

Arriving at the landing, he could hear a romantic flute coming from the bedroom. This immediately gave him another kick on his already steep ascent into heaven.

Heartily, he sang, 'Oh, Meghan, my sweetest sweetheart, your hairy bear is so prepared for you,' and walked into the bedroom. He placed his bag beside the bed and anxiously started to unpack the items he had bought.

In the gloom, he could not see where exactly Meghan was lying as his eyes were still adjusting to the darkness. Clumsy as he was, he fumbled around on the bed, unfortunately directly hitting one of Meghan's ears. He apologised. After a few more touches he could make out her face, placed a soft kiss on her forehead, lifted her head a few inches up in the air and immediately tied the silky blindfold over her eyes. Meghan was so excited she was only able to make a few grunts of surprise, as everything came so unexpectedly.

Harry went back to his secret shopping trophies. This time he grabbed the flogger and started to tease Meghan down her long, shaved legs. With that Meghan slowly started to move around as the sensation was very itchy, yet exciting.

Harry realised that this was not what he wanted. He wanted her to keep still. That way, he could tease her much more intensively with the flogger. With a clear and deep voice, he commanded, 'Keep still, otherwise I'll have to punish you.'

Meghan giggled like a teenager and abruptly stopped moving on the sheet.

Harry quickly took his next surprise tool and made a few awkward grabs until he found Meghan's hand. As she was too far away from where he intended her to be, he took her hand and made her understand she was to move towards the head of the bed. Meghan did so without rebelling, curious to know what he had planned. Before long, she heard a sudden click and found she was already handcuffed to one of the tall wooden bedposts. Before she had time to work out whether she liked that or not, her second hand was fixed to the opposite post.

When Harry got down to one of her feet and realised that she was wearing boots, he let out a cry of sudden ecstasy, which made Meghan smile. She had clearly made the right decision.

When Harry had finally finished, the boots squeezed into the handcuffs at their widest point with lots of effort, Meghan lay there, spread like someone who had been lying in the sun for too long, trying to cool down from the heat. The lights from a car driving by allowed a quick glimpse of his adorable Meghan as she was stretched there, handcuffed, dressed in sexy underwear and wearing her shiny rubber boots. What a sight! What excitement! Harry was almost not capable of containing himself any longer. Therefore, he quickly took off his underpants to fan a bit of fresh air to his nose, knowing that Meghan was not able to see what was going on.

Now that his 'victim' lay there, all prepared, he could begin his sweet torture. He started licking the bottoms of her sweet, soft wellies, slowly making his way up to her knees and continuing further across her well-trained tummy towards her perfect breasts.

It was right before he reached her moist lips that a huge

explosion outside the cottage made Harry jump almost to the ceiling. Meghan was still blindfolded and, the cloth also covering her ears, her hearing was slightly impaired. For her, the explosion sounded far more distant.

Meghan was sure that this was part of the kidnap training. She laughed. 'Oh, Harry, my sweetie, I am really getting frightened ...'

Harry, on the other hand, was utterly shocked; what the hell was going on outside? By now only wearing one of his in-need-of-replacement socks, he hurried downstairs and drew the window-mirror to one side. He could see a soldier in full uniform standing in front of the door.

Only seconds later, the bell was ringing. Harry turned around, his sweaty back against the door, his hands spread against the wood as if this would help to prevent anyone from entering. His mind was at light-speed as he gasped for air.

A few minutes passed. Another ring knocked Harry almost out of his only sock. Oh, goodness! What should he do? He despaired.

Upstairs, Meghan started to call for him.

A loud and very demanding banging on the door, accompanied by a firm voice shouting, 'We know you are in here,' made Harry almost stumble across to the umbrella stand, but with only a few steps he stood safely in the kitchen. It was not the first time he was glad to have such a tiny home. He grabbed the kitchen towel and tied it around his hips.

The soldier outside was prepared to lift his hand for another heavy knock on the door when a flushed Harry opened it, grinning all over his face, twittering nonchalantly: 'Oh, hello, how are you?'

'Sorry, sir, we have been ordered to evacuate the whole place immediately.'

'Whattttt?' Harry screamed in such an uncontrolled and high-pitched way that the soldier immediately had to hold his hand to his closer ear.

'Sir, it's an order. Everybody in the house has to evacuate now. Instantly.'

'I don't give a—'

The soldier was just able to grab the door and put his foot in the gap before Harry could slam it. 'Sir, we have a dangerous intruder warning on the grounds of Kensington Palace. It's the Queen's command to evacuate everybody immediately. You have two minutes before we storm your place!'

Having made his statement, the soldier turned around, leaving a pale Harry looking like a white bedsheet standing in the doorframe. He was in such a paralysed state that his muscles didn't work any more and he let the kitchen towel sink to the ground.

Another explosion, which was much closer, hit him out of his shock. He accelerated so quickly that he lost his last sock right by the entrance and rushed as if the devil were after him up the stairs, crying, 'Meeeeeghan, we have to evacuaaaate!'

He almost slipped on the carpet as he slid around the corner into the bedroom, finding Meghan licking her lips.

'Of course, Harry, we have to do this,' she said, with a long chuckle.

Harry was almost out of his mind. 'No, Meghie, this is serious, we are under attack!'

'Oh, again?'

'Yes, this time for real!' Harry was desperately trying to

find the keys for the handcuffs. 'Where the hell are they?' he muttered to himself. 'Where did I put them?'

A loud knock downstairs only made him tenser, his hands shaking vigorously as if being greeted by Mr Trump. Speeding around in the tiny bedroom, Harry hit one of the bedposts with his hairy toe and screamed. Meghan started to get high-strung, realising that something was definitely going wrong.

Downstairs, the door could be heard cracking from being opened with force. Harry's face went from white to ashen; luckily it was pitch dark and nobody could see it. He could tell with certainty by now that it had to be serious.

Meghan was getting increasingly nervous as she was not able to see anything or hear properly. 'Haaarry, what's going on?'

'Don't worry, darling, all good—'

Suddenly another loud bang was heard, the bedroom door flew open and the troops of the emergency unit rushed in. The suddenly switched-on light tortured Harry's eyes into blindness for a few seconds.

By now, Harry and Meghan were crying in stereo while troops whirled around the bed like the inhabitants of a hectic anthill. Everybody joined the screaming, interleaved with military commands that went unheard, while Harry and Meghan were screaming louder to emphasise their miserable situation. This continued until the commander of the troop stopped in front of Harry and grabbed him by his ginger chest hair, forcing him to open his eyes and look into the commander's.

'Where are the handcuff keys, sir?' the commander yelled at Harry, at such a volume that the few hairs on

Harry's head flew backwards in the wind his voice generated.

'That's the problem; I don't knoooooow, sir,' Harry shouted back, his Adam's apple vibrating enormously, some veins standing out in his neck.

The officer, stomping his boot to raise attention, shouted, 'Get hold of the lady; we have to lift her up until the handcuffs get over the top of the bedposts!'

Harry summoned up his courage, forgot about military hierarchy, clicked his heels and hurt himself awfully as he was barefoot. 'Everybody at their place; I'll couuuunt,' he shouted.

All the soldiers gathered around the bed, some of them kneeling on the sheet, a bit embarrassed but at the same time aroused by the unexpected vision in front of their eyes. Harry started to count.

'One ...'

Another explosion outside made the bed shake vigorously. Meghan's cries were growing more desperate.

'Two ...'

Beads of perspiration were starting to appear on the foreheads of the strained soldiers.

There was another close bang just outside the window.

'Threeeeee ...'

And with a grunting roar of effort everybody started to lift Meghan, supporting her from underneath, the soldiers having to place their hands on delicate body parts, looking away to take the bite out of the situation. As they lifted her up, inch by inch, Meghan suddenly started to scream wildly:

'Ah, you are hurting me!'

The tension of the four handcuffs had become

unbearable, as the posts curved outwards towards the top, making the pulling hurt more with every inch she was lifted. Alarmed by her pain, the soldiers suddenly let go and Meghan came thundering down onto the bedsheet.

'Everyone back at their plaaaaace,' Harry cried. 'We'll have another try. One ...' everybody grunting, 'two ...' everybody panting, 'threeeeee ...' everybody almost fainting ...

Again, only a few inches from freedom, Meghan cried out, her wrists sore from the constant chafing of the tight handcuffs. This time, her falling back wasn't that soft, as one of the soldiers let go too quickly. The lifting operation was thrown out of balance and with that the whole formation tipped to the side where the soldier had let go, causing the others to let go as well. With a sudden crash, Meghan fell down to the mattress screaming as if sharks were trying to bite off her extremities.

Both Harry and the commander were also screaming, albeit for a different reason.

Meghan's state made any further attempt to lift her out of her misery a non-starter. A flash of desperation struck through everybody's bones, challenging even war-proven soldiers. What could be done?

Suddenly the commander had a very bright idea: 'Get a saw!'

While the words were still fading away, Harry had already stormed out wearing Meghan's trousers, which were the only thing he had been able to quickly find. He was overstretching them with every step he took as he sped downstairs, out into the garden, into the shed. Fumbling like a madman in the chaos of the tools, he finally found an old and rusty saw. He was immediately heading back, almost losing the now-torn trousers, slipping on his lost sock at the entrance, speeding back up to the bedroom. Completely out of breath, he handed the saw to the commander.

'Start sawing, with interchaaaange!' the commander yelled, and the first soldier started to saw, almost breaking the rusty tool, as the bedpost was so thick. He handed the saw quickly over to the next in the row, the second one not doing much better.

After three turns of handing over the old metal blade the sawing soldier suddenly hit something that produced a shrill sound, making everybody cover their ears. When he put down the saw some very shiny metal appeared under the wood.

'Oh, no, it's a metal frame, disguised as wood!' Harry gasped, and everybody sunk onto their knees with a common sigh. Desperation and hopelessness were in the air, leaving everybody to drown in self-pity.

'Everybody can leave. I'll stay with the sinking ship,' Harry announced miserably. Meghan was sobering with every word.

As the soldiers were getting ready to give in, starting to prepare for leaving, a very loud shouting could be heard from downstairs.

The commander's face turned pale pink; his voice faded out into a desperate whisper. 'They are coming.'

Meghan's blubbering made her chest rise and fall quickly, competing with the shaking lace of her bra.

Some dragging steps up the stairs were audible, making the tension unbearable. Each soldier had his own way to face the unavoidable situation. Some of them prayed their seemingly last prayer and asked for forgiveness; others thought of what they had missed in their lives, while others were just full of self-loathing for having been enough of a fool to become a professional soldier. Harry thought of a last refreshing sip of cold beer. Everybody stuck their heads in their hands, in their arms or between their knees. Only Meghan was not able to hide her face as she was still bound to the four bedposts.

Into the room Prince Philip stuck his big nose, sporting a fleshy wart on the tip of it, grinning all over his face, his cheeks reddish from excitement.

'How was that?' he asked with a thundering voice. 'How did you like the emergency drill? Was it close enough to reality?' He turned Harry. 'I hope you didn't mind me spicing things up a little bit.'

The specialist task force hadn't been informed that Prince Philip had secretly arranged an emergency drill, thus making everybody believe it was a real situation. Since stalkers had intruded on the royal grounds before, everybody knew how dangerous they could get. The royals needed training from time to time to keep them alert, and it was better for nobody to know, so it would feel more serious.

A common sigh of relief swept through the whole of Nottingham Cottage. A few soldiers blacked out, falling to the side, like balloons from which the air had been let out.

The Kid's Birthday Party

Harry loved children above all, and with Meghan he had found a woman who joined him in enjoying every moment he was able to spend with kids. This deepened his love for this beautiful woman in such a tremendous way that sometimes he was not sure whether he loved her or the children more.

Luckily, another birthday was coming up. This time it was that of a friend of little Charlotte, the second child of Harry's brother William and his wife Kate, at whose house the party was going to be held. As it was the first kid's birthday Meghan would be able to attend with funcle Harry, Harry's toes started to prickle days before the event. It was so exciting to think he could soon introduce Meghan to the funny games he played with the kids and could show her what a great dad he would be himself.

Harry started to get into his best form. A few days before the event he thrust himself into preparations such as shopping for presents, buying balloons, getting fireworks and ordering a special birthday cake at Harrods, with the birthday girl's name iced in pink letters between fondant unicorns. As a special attraction he bought some fancy paints for the skin, intending to make a face painting workshop in the garden.

Of course, he mentioned none of this to Kate or William. He wanted to surprise everybody, making full use of his title as a funcle. Harry would have given a lot to be a kid on this day. He liked to adopt the carefree nature of the kids, laughing and giggling with them, forgetting about rules and royalty for a few hours.

Harry and Meghan were standing in front of stately and impressive Anmer Hall on this unusually warm early winter day. With great effort the heavy door was opened by Charlotte herself, her tiny face filled with laughter, showing some dimples on her cheeks that blushed with anticipation. She was dressed in a white summer dress, with little pink flowers spread all over the chiffon. She looked like a princess and Harry immediately lifted her up, kissed her and let her sit on his arm.

*

After half of the cake had been smeared across the entire sofa, the face paints generously applied on Lupo (who had suddenly fled the scene, howling loudly), the presents wildly torn open, wrapping paper flying all over the reception room. Harry took Meghan by the hand, whisking her secretly to the conservatory where he had placed the material for his evening show. Outside, it was already dusk: the perfect time to start preparations for the fireworks.

But before that, he wanted to get the kids' balloons ready. His plan was to fix a small candle below a funnel with an air valve at the end of the balloons, which would cause the air underneath to heat up and therefore enable the balloons to fly. The light from the candles would make the balloons glow while flying out into the night; they could have the kids think about their secret wishes while letting go of them.

Harry could barely wait any more to start work on his

surprise. All kid himself, he danced from one foot to the other, very keen on explaining to Meghan how she could help him. For his candle idea, he had bought extra-durable balloons which were more hard-wearing, but also tougher to inflate.

At the same time, Kate was looking for missing Lupo, poor dog. He always suffered from too many children. She would be glad for him when the party was over. She had already searched the whole house without finding him, and her steps finally took her to the conservatory, the last part of the house before she would have to search the garden.

The conservatory was at the far end of the house. She had to pass through a long hallway, where she first had to switch on the lights, as it was getting dark fast. Behind her the noise of the screaming kids faded out, and Kate was glad to get a bit of fresh air and silence herself. She loved children very much, but such a birthday party could be very strenuous and she was looking forward to a quieter evening.

Continuing her walk down the hallway, Kate heard some voices in the distance, seemingly coming from the conservatory. She had not expected anyone here at this time. Frowning, she accelerated her walk, trying to prevent any treacherous noise, and approached the door that was around the corner. In order to avoid confrontation, Kate stopped right before the corner and turned off the light, listening anxiously to the voices behind the wall.

'Oh, Meghan, you have to put more effort in ... you must blow harder, otherwise it will never work!'

Meghan was gasping for air. 'Harder? How? I am already out of breath ...'

Some heavy breathing was audible . . .

Harry groaned. 'Don't let anything flow back; just blow, blow more!'

Kate put her hand to her mouth in shock, her eyes widening.

'Oh, darling, try harder. It just needs more pressure!'

Silence.

'Meghan, it has to grow more; it is just not good enough for us to go on to the next step. I'll help you hold it.' Harry's moaning intensified, seemingly under great tension.

A cry almost escaped from Kate's mouth. This was incredible; how did they dare to do that here? At a children's party! What if a kid accidentally bumped into the scene? Horrific images started to rise in Kate's mind.

'Harry, I can't any more. You have to try yourself; maybe you can do it better yourself! I've never been good at blowing these things.'

That was it; enough. Kate, suppressing a yell, whirled around and bumped directly into a large, soft bosom; Camilla had turned up unexpectedly behind her, looking for some fresh air and distraction from the kids' chaos. Kate's face was deep purple by now and, at the last second, she managed to place her finger on Camilla's mouth, preventing her from making any noise. Together, hand in hand, they approached to listen again.

'What do you mean, you have never been good at blowing these things?' Harry demanded. 'Why didn't you tell me before? What's this now? Do you mean I have to do it myself? I am already busy getting the ropes ready for tying. Try again; you need to get it larger.'

Silence.

A cry of joy escaped Harry's mouth. 'Ah, Meghan, that's much better. The sooner it's ready, the sooner it will lift up, for a reeaal niiice taaaake-ooooff.' The last few words were slowly drawn out. Harry was not able to suppress his anticipation.

The air was prickling.

Meghan spoke, panting. 'My cheeks are already hurting from the constant in and out. I am really sorry; I can't continue like this.'

The large fascinator on Camilla's head almost lifted up in the air, such a great heat wave emanated from her overwhelming shock.

'But it needs more work and more intense blowing,' Harry said. 'Otherwise it won't be big enough, the thing will never lift, and there will be no fun.'

The moaning was in gunshot mode by now. Camilla fumbled nervously in her handbag.

'Why don't you take one hand and press your cheeks together?' Harry asked. 'Like this. You will blow straight from your throat without blowing up your cheeks.'

Meghan was panting louder, seemingly under great effort.

By this point, even Camilla couldn't stand it any longer. With a trained and elegant movement she brought out her inflatable toilet seat, ready to inflate here and now. Kate, seeing what Camilla was up to, was hardly able to hinder her from her intention.

'This is so much easier now; it flows so much easier,' Meghan said.

'Oh, darling, you did it! Ah, finally,' Harry exclaimed with great excitement. 'One more blow and it will be at its peak! Yeahhhh, push it a bit more, baby.'

Kate was as stiff as if she had swallowed a stick, not showing any movement on her anxious face.

'Oh, Meghie, sweetheart, you've made it so big it's about to explode!'

Sounds of pain and exhaustion emerged from Meghan's mouth. 'Finally, it seems I got the trick,' she managed to say. 'Let me just give it one more blow.'

'Meghan, stop now, please! It will soon explode! Stop it now!'

The two women in the hallway were submerged in the darkest nightmare of their lives, tightly holding each other's hands with one hand and their handbags with the other, eyes pressed shut in despair. They whirled around together in one movement and bumped into Charles, who had come along in search of some fresh air and quiet, without having a clue about what was going on.

'It's Meghan and Harry,' Camilla whispered to Charles. 'It would appear that they are doing it in the conservatory.'

Looking at their horror-filled, frightened faces, Charles was about to join their gallop back to the drawing room when a huge explosion was heard coming from the conservatory.

Profound silence.

After a seeming eternity a ripping sound came from the conservatory. Charles's eyes widened, a sudden painful memory rising in his head; he was sent back to Nottingham Cottage. A quick check in his pocket reassured him that he had his inflatable device to hand whenever needed.

A sudden scream inside the conservatory catapulted everybody out of their shock and back into reality. Three pairs of eyes were at their largest opening possible.

'For heaven's sake, Meghan, what have you done? It's broken; it's your mistake! Can't blow up this one any more.'

'No Harry, stop this now; it is your mistake. I blew as hard as I could, but you should not have held it so tight when I tried to tie the rope around the outlet.'

Charles's ears were now showing clearly that he was feeling very uneasy. They were of the most intense violet shade Camilla had ever seen on him. The tension was unbearable.

The ping-pong shouting from the conservatory turned into stereo, argumentative screaming when another unforeseen explosion happened and brought the situation to a climax. Swept up in the moment, the three listeners in the hallway joined in the screaming, in a rather frightened way – first Kate, then Camilla, then Charles – which caused Harry's and Meghan's yelling to pitch even higher, unsure of what the sudden chaos and screaming from the hallway would mean.

With all five screaming and yelling together at different heights, they could even be heard far back in the drawing room, where the talking, kidding and laughing came to a sudden halt. William's face fell and, together with Prince Philip, he ran as if Lucifer were chasing him to the cellar, where they could prepare for the worst.

Once back upstairs, the two army-proven men, now in full armour and equipped with heavy guns, sneaked down the corridor towards the conservatory. Horror was painted on the Queen's face while the children gathered around her in fear. Anmer Hall had to have been invaded by intruders.

With smooth and soundless steps, William and Philip approached the ongoing screaming, coming closer to the conservatory. At last they turned the corner and found themselves facing Kate, Camilla and Charles, huddled up and trembling in the centre of the hallway, their faces blue from screaming. As the armed men were spotted, not recognisable under their camouflage, the three started to scream louder, making the screaming in the conservatory rise as well.

In a last attempt to get the desperate situation under control, Philip lifted the gun and fired a warning shot out of the window into the dark night, causing everybody to fall silent immediately. Smoke coming out of his gun barrel, Philip lifted his helmet, making it clear to everybody it was him. He stood there with a grim face as the conservatory door opened.

A most astonished Harry and Meghan stepped out, with Meghan squeaking, 'What's going on? We were just trying to blow up some balloons for the children when a couple of them exploded.'

Shooting at Sandringham

The end of the year presented itself in its most beautiful dress, the leaves having turned to show all possible shades between yellow, orange, red and violet, converting the city parks into an endless explosion of colours. Meghan was fascinated by this spectacle. The mist lying like a soft carpet over the grass gave the scenery a mystic touch and, when she walked with her dog under the trees, she loved the sound of the rustling leaves under her marching feet. In the countryside, the first thin layer of snow had thrown a big white blanket over the hills and across the valleys.

Around this time, Harry announced that his grandmother, the Queen, had invited both of them for the annual gathering at Sandringham House, including the Christmas dinner and the traditional shooting.

Meghan was excited. This was a welcome chance to make, once and for all, an outstanding impression in front of the gathered royal family and in front of the Queen, especially after her last few blunders.

Meghan didn't know much about shooting, except that it was a men's sport. She assumed the ladies stayed behind in nicely decorated houses while the men were out in the fields. She favoured that idea since she was not thrilled about shooting, being an ardent animal lover. As long as she didn't have to witness the killing, it would be OK.

She imagined the ladies would be looking forward to celebrating their men's trophies, perhaps even more than the men would. They would probably have a chat, holding a bubbly drink in front of a warm log fire in the elegant reception room of a castle or country house, waiting for the tired men to bring home their prey.

Meghan was equipped with a suitable dress for Christmas but still needed a proper outfit for the shooting day. To make herself fit for the occasion, she had decided to go on a shopping tour, visiting the best designers in New Bond Street. As a dressing guideline she had images of great splendour from Royal Ascot in her mind. She intended to surprise everybody, including Harry, and therefore didn't say a word about what she was planning.

As they packed for the long weekend, Harry asked Meghan, 'Honey, sweetheart, shall I give you a hand with packing everything you'll need?'

'No, Harry Bear, I already did, thank you. I have prepared well and I want to impress everybody.' She blinked her eyes and enchanted him with her sweetest smile.

Harry raised one eyebrow, but he knew Meghan was always thoroughly prepared and he therefore didn't oppose her.

'Meghie, where are your suitcases?' he asked as they packed the car, the boot being almost full of his own bulky luggage.

'Oh, this is it,' Meghan chirped, handing him her oversized beauty case and a rather small piece of luggage suitable for an overnight stay.

'Is this all?' Harry asked, his doubts rising.

She giggled. 'Yeah. It's a surprise.'

Harry wondered, but maybe she really *was* being surprising; maybe she had already arranged for her clothes to be delivered directly to Sandringham itself. He smiled and shook his head, curious about what might happen later.

It was in the early morning of Christmas Eve, and the two lovers sat in Harry's Jeep with great anticipation and an accelerated heartbeat. With a swift manoeuvre Harry set the car off for the coming weekend, his warm left hand placed on Meghan's well-shaved, bare upper leg, her miniskirt allowing him complete and unhindered access.

When they arrived before midday at imposing and splendid Sandringham, everybody was in the best of moods. Since Meghan had never been on a shoot before, special arrangements had been made for an introductory shooting session in the afternoon.

After the butler had shown Harry and Meghan to their magnificent room, Harry was quick to go outside, looking to see whether his hand was needed for final shooting preparations. Meghan was completely on her own, unpacking – which was a quick thing – and changing clothes. Checking her outfit in the extravagant full-length, gold-framed mirror, she was satisfied with the outcome of her time-consuming preparations. Nothing could go wrong this time. With a cheerful whistle on her lips she headed down to the reception room, where everybody was supposed to gather in a few minutes.

Down she walked, descending the wide staircase to the grand entrance hall in her stunning dress. The fabric made a promising sound as it rustled with every step she took. She felt so good, so wanted and so special. She would surely throw the other ladies into the shade.

It almost knocked Harry out of his thick woollen hunting socks when she entered the room. He was absolutely hypnotised by her appearance. But what was this? Was she dressed for a gala dinner? The dress was elegant, and seemingly endless fabric floated around her beautiful slim legs; she was wearing long, white silk gloves, as actresses used to in the best days of Hollywood. Harry, unable to say a word while his beard hair lifted up from astonishment, made a rewarding grunting sound, looking rather proudly at his Meghan.

Glancing quickly through the room, a bit nervous, Meghan realised that everybody was already there, having some welcome drinks. She could make out a few ladies, but most of them still seemed to be dressed casually. Hiding her smile, she thought to herself, *Well, not everybody is as well prepared as I am. I am an exception, I know. The other ladies just haven't planned well, if they're still wearing their dog walking outfits for their welcome drinks.*

She was proud of sporting the correct dress, and the stunned glances rewarded her with more self-confidence. As she was introduced to all the guests, Meghan noticed to her surprise that she was in fact the only lady who had already changed for the event. This made her carry her bosom with an even more upright back.

She chuckled when Harry took her to one side.

'Darling,' he whispered in her ear, 'you look stunning, but when do you plan to change? It will soon be time to leave.'

Meghan was very surprised. 'But, Harry Bear, I *have* changed.'

'Into this? For shooting?'

'What do you mean, shooting?' Meghan asked. '*You* go shooting, not me!'

'My sweetie, you join us. You are supposed to come with us. You are invited, invited to *shoot*!'

Meghan had started to realise that somebody must have misunderstood something but was not quite ready to consider herself a candidate. 'No, I stay with the ladies.'

'Of course you can stay with the ladies, but you'll still need some proper country wear, because all the ladies will join the shoot!'

It was now that Meghan blushed in the same colour as the thick red velvet curtains of the reception room. 'Harry, this is *all* I brought with me, except for the nightie!'

Harry stared at her, complete incomprehension on his worried face. 'Oh my God, Meghan, what were you thinking? Didn't you know? We go *hunting*, or *shooting*, whatever you want to call it. We go out in the fields. The formal dinner is later!'

Meghan, now totally out of control, rushed off to the ladies' room. She needed to hide and think of how to escape her misery.

In the hallway she bumped into the Queen.

'Oh, Meghan,' Her Majesty said, 'this is a stunning dress. I understand you want to wear it as early as you can. But I do expect you to be ready in a few minutes when the announcement is to be made with all the shooting instructions.'

Meghan was deep purple by now. 'Of course, ma'am, I'll do my best!'

And off she hurried, almost falling into the bathroom, with such effort had she stormed into it. There she gasped for air.

A moment later, Princess Eugenie entered the room. Meghan could do nothing other than tell her everything about her disastrous situation.

Eugenie was not able to understand every detail between all the sobbing that came out of Meghan's deep red lipstick-covered mouth, but she gathered the overall situation. As she was a regular at Sandringham for certain events, it happened that she had quite a few country wardrobe items that she would keep at the house. She hurried off to look for some appropriate stuff. After a few minutes, she came back, almost matching Meghan's breathlessness, carrying some tweed clothes under her arm.

'This is the only halfway suitable outfit I could find so quickly. Go and check whether it fits you,' she gasped.

Meghan almost ripped off part of her never-ending dress in the doorframe as she slammed the toilet door behind her. After a very hurried change, the sweat dripping down her face making her once-dramatic makeup run in streaks, she walked out of the cubicle.

Eugenie had to try hard not to burst out in laughter. The trousers were much too short, as Meghan was taller, but at the same time they were too loose, as Meghan was slimmer. Meghan looked a perfect fool. And, without a belt, there was no chance the trousers would actually stay on her waist.

'Well, it'll do for the emergency, but I have seen better outfits on you,' Eugenie said, half-laughing, without intending any malice.

After a long silence, while the two ladies were very embarrassed, Eugenie added, 'To be honest, Meghan, it looks terrible, I am afraid to say.'

Meghan was in a state of despair. Hope was sinking, and had actually already reached her slim ankles, when suddenly she saw the bright flash of a superb idea. What would she do without her preparation skills? Having learnt from former mistakes, she was now always prepared for the worst. Quickly, she grabbed her clutch and disappeared into the toilet again, leaving Eugenie wondering what had stung poor Meghan.

From inside the cubicle the sound of air under pressure could be heard, which left Eugenie even more embarrassed. She was about to leave the ladies' room, in order to avoid being exposed to further disgraceful sounds, when Meghan opened the door in a great swing, laughing from one ear to another, and stepped out of the toilet cubicle. Brimming with pride, she turned around and showed Eugenie her back, the trousers now sitting tight as if tailor-made.

Eugenie's eyeballs were at the point of exploding; never had she seen anything similar. Meghan now sported a full and impressive backside close to Kim Kardashian's famous behind, all made possible thanks to a half-inflated toilet seat stuffed into the too-big trousers. Wow, this was a sight. Eugenie was more than overwhelmed, speechlessly giving Meghan her approval by showing her an upright thumb.

Meghan's self-confidence was reset. As she walked out of the bathroom, she tried to keep her attitude as bright as possible. With her unusually swollen behind, walking was a bit awkward and waggling her hips somehow needed more power, but after a few steps Meghan got the right swing.

She re-entered the reception room and found herself

faced by a group of people who were only too keen to look at her, full of expectation. It was dead silent and the only sound that could be heard was the clacking of her tremendous high heels on the wooden floor; she had not replaced them with any more suitable footwear. It was embarrassing at best.

Nobody said a word. Most of the guests tried to avoid the situation by looking at the highly decorated ceiling or let their eyes rove out of the window into the beautiful garden. The only people who directly looked for eye contact were the Queen and Harry. The Queen's face was rather unapproachable, but Harry formed his mouth into the shape of words in slow motion, grimacing through his hairy beard. He looked like he was trying to mouth, *Meghan, why? What's that?*

Her shaky catwalk over the slippery, freshly oiled wooden floor to the other guests felt like an eternity, and inside Meghan died a few deaths. Finally reaching Harry, she was barely able to keep herself upright, her knees feeling like marshmallows cooked on an open fire. With the innocent look of a fawn, she blinked with her fake long eyelashes, murmuring to Harry, 'Better?'

Harry was simultaneously tempted to look approvingly at her enlarged backside and completely at a loss. 'Meghan, what about your shoes?'

Meghan's face fell. Oh, goodness, she had completely forgotten about that part! Gulping as if she were swallowing a stone, she replied, 'Not here, darling ...'

Harry's face was greyer than hers by now, but he could not ask any more questions, as the sign was given to leave and everybody started to move.

*

Once everyone had been driven in Land Rovers to the hunting grounds, Meghan, still in her high heels, was almost unable to keep up with the pace of the marching group, everyone else naturally in booted gear. Not wanting to fall behind, she tried speeding up, but this did not make her move any faster; it just made her movements look worse. When she took a step with greater speed and therefore weight, her high heels tended to sink deeper into the moist ground, slowing her down each time she had to pull the heels out again. She nearly fell over a few times, making Harry impatient as he watched her. When the rest of the group was in front of them, watching Prince Philip raise his gun to aim at his first target, Harry stopped by Meghan's side and quietly snapped, 'Off with them!'

Meghan immediately obliged; she would be happy to get rid of these terrible murder heels. She bent down to remove them in a quick movement, which, to her misfortune, brought the situation to bursting point. Not capable of bearing the pressure any further, her tightly squeezed toilet seat blew up with a big bang.

Thinking that a shot had been fired behind them, the entire group trembled as if struck by a terrifying seizure. Some of the people, especially men who had done military service, threw themselves to the ground, thinking they might be attacked. Prince Philip was so startled that he pulled the trigger in his shock. As the rules demanded, everybody had stayed behind the front gun, and therefore luckily his blind shot did not do any harm to anyone. No one realised that the bullet had hit one of the Land Rovers, which were parked some distance away. The shot had drilled itself directly into a tyre and started to slowly flatten it.

Meanwhile, unobserved by anyone, Meghan threw her shoes into a nearby bush.

After everybody had recovered, not able to determine where exactly the first shot had come from, the leader of the hunt called Harry and Meghan to come closer to the group. He had concluded that there might be an unannounced neighbouring shooting party in the area and didn't want to take the risk of someone being hurt by a misfired shot. He started to lead the party away, keeping an eye on Meghan, and, when no one was listening, said to her, 'Ahem, Meghan, you didn't misfire, I hope. You must be very careful, especially as a beginner!'

Meghan walked with large strides next to the leader, now that she did not bore holes into the ground with each step any more. Harry, a few steps behind, saw to his utmost shock that her tweed trousers showed a great slit. They must have torn when she was bending down to take off her heels. And out of the trousers hung pieces of rubber from the blown-up toilet seat.

Harry had a serious attack of near-fainting. It was too late; Meghan was ahead of the group, with everyone catching up and some of the guests wondering what on earth she carried in her trousers. A few more quick steps allowed Harry to walk closely behind her and prevent the worst by holding up her loose trousers, his embarrassment growing by the second.

The leader of the group was quite adamant that the only way Meghan would come to understand the rules of shooting was by doing some shooting herself. Unfortunately, her opposition was not going to be heard.

After a short introduction to how to handle a gun, Meghan stood there, raising the gun, hesitating to press the trigger as she was afraid of it. After a few awkward moments had passed, the leader asked her to fire her first shot. She closed her eyes so tightly it was almost painful and pulled the trigger. Without any clue what she was doing, she let the shot leave the gun. Not knowing that Murphy's Law also applied when shooting, she directly hit another tyre of the very same Land Rover. The damage was undetectable, though, with the tyres losing air very slowly.

Much to Meghan's relief and surprise, the hunting leader was satisfied with her first shot and left her alone from then on. But her true misery was only about to begin. She still had to walk in her stockings. The rough grass stuck sharply into her delicate feet and she could hardly suppress a few cries as it hurt her so much. Her nylons were soaked from the damp ground. Harry's comment on her exploded trousers only added to her pain. The planned march was a long one and the shoot was to be particularly extended as an extra welcoming gesture from the Queen to newcomer Meghan.

After the lengthy torture of a seemingly endless shoot, the group finally made it back to the car park, where everybody dispersed into their vehicles, glad to have a seat. Meghan was the very last one to get back, almost unable to walk upright any more, her feet covered with blisters and bloody scratches. The other cars had already left.

Harry was at the end of his nerves. The entire ordeal had stretched his patience. He liked to attract attention with Meghan, but not like this! He almost had to push her into the car from behind.

When the driver started the engine and tried to drive off, the tyre failure became clear.

'I'm afraid to say that we have two flat tyres,' the driver announced, 'and, with only one spare and no mobile phone coverage here to call for help, we'll have to walk back!'

Climbing out of the car again was the end for Meghan. In a last desperate attempt to keep herself upright, she grabbed for Harry's arm, but she almost blacked out before finding it and sank to the ground. When she opened her tired eyes again, she whispered into Harry's most concerned face, 'My hairy Harry, I am too exhausted to walk; please leave me in the car.'

As some very dark clouds were assembling and rain was threatening, it was not a good idea to leave her behind and pick her up later. In this miserable situation, the sunken hero recovered and Harry's army instincts rose. 'All men at my commaaaaand, make the guns ready!' he screamed, his neck widening with the effort.

Everybody was alarmed to consider what crazy Harry might be thinking. He was not going to shoot his own lady, was he? Horrified, the three men who had shared the car with them reported to his side. All eyes were on him.

'The meeen with the biggest waxed coats,' Harry commanded, 'take them off and bind them around the guns.'

Was he combining the shooting with a funeral ritual, using the coats as flags? Nobody dared to move.

A few unbearable moments passed, the tension growing.

Harry finally spoke again. 'Connect and bind the ends of the waxed clothes together; form a rescuuue stretcher!'

A common sigh of relief swept through the Midlands. The stretcher was formed quickly and poor Meghan was lifted onto it to be carried back.

Swinging back and forth as she was carried, Meghan almost had to throw up from the earlier drinks she had had. She could hardly endure any more.

Back at Sandringham, the worried Queen and the crowd gathered in front of the big entrance door, anxious to welcome the lost group back. With the last of her dignity and power, Meghan was able to drag herself out of the stretcher and raise herself with the help of Harry. With a painful, not overly well-acted artificial smile, she passed the crowd.

As soon as she was out of everyone's eyeshot, Meghan fell on her knees and crept up the stairs on her fours back to their room. Inside, she burst into tears. After Harry had taken off her socks under waves of shrieks, he looked with pity at her tortured feet. They were very miserable indeed.

When treating her feet, Harry glanced over them, thinking that she deserved nicer feet as their shape was not the best, and instructed her, 'Meghan, from now on, you carry boots with you wherever you go. This is England, not California. Wearing wellies to the wrong occasion is still better than wearing high heels to the wrong occasion.'

Harry was almost as exhausted as his girlfriend. They both deliberately missed dinner.

Harry's command kept sticking in Meghan's brain, and she swore never to be in another situation where she lacked boots. This would have later consequences, not known to Harry yet. But for now, she closed her eyes and drifted away in a dreamless deep sleep. She woke up early the next morning, when the sun was just about to rise.

When Meghan sat up in bed, it took her a moment to realise where she was, but soon her mind brought unwelcome memories back. She was quickly thrown back into a similar state of desperation to yesterday afternoon. What were all the guests thinking of her? And then the Queen? What were they going to do with her today? According to the Queen, yesterday had only been an 'introductory day', a 'soft and slow warm-up'.

Horror started to rise as Meghan imagined the up-coming day. She had to get herself prepared. Most importantly, she absolutely needed some wellies!

When she placed her wounded feet on the soft carpet and tried to stand up, a hiss of pain escaped her dry mouth. Terrified, she turned to check whether Harry had woken up, but luckily he was still fast asleep, some heavy snoring making his nostrils wobble. She grabbed her 'turn-off' fleece slippers, well-hidden underneath the bed, and on velvet paws she sneaked out and headed down, Sandringham House still very much asleep.

The house was huge and quite a maze, with endless hallways and rooms. But somehow Meghan was able to find what she was looking for. She had a good sense of orientation and therefore, after only a few bad tries when she opened a wrong door, she managed to find the Queen's boot room. There she hoped to find a pair of fitting wellies she could secretly borrow.

Just as she had been hoping, the Queen had a whole range of boots. Joyfully, Meghan grabbed a pair and nicely rearranged the remaining boots to leave no gap and no trace. This way, her borrowing for the day would not be detected.

Quickly and under pressure, afraid that somebody might enter unexpectedly, she eagerly sat down on the bench and pulled the first boot on over her sock. It seemed to be too small, although she thought she had taken what had looked like the largest pair. Her feet had probably swollen by two or more sizes overnight. In her despair, Meghan pulled harder, trying to squeeze in. She absolutely needed a pair to survive the new day!

At that moment, Meghan's face froze to ice. In the distance, echoing from the hallway's old stones, she clearly could hear footsteps coming closer.

In panic, Meghan pulled harder; she needed to get the boots on as taking them off no longer had a reasonable chance of success. What if someone happened to enter the boot room and saw her here? Sweat was building up on her forehead. Stuck at the ankle, she was neither able to slip into the boot completely nor to pull back out of it. Meghan was terrified and in agony as the boot pressed firmly against her blisters.

The steps stopped in front of the boot room's door. She could clearly hear the Queen's voice, talking to another person. 'Yes, thank you very much. I shall come back to you when I have returned from the early morning dog walk.'

Her eyes at least as big as her anxiety by now, Meghan remembered having been told the Queen insisted on walking the dogs in the fresh early morning air at Sandringham before anyone else got up. How could she have forgotten?

In pure panic her eyes scanned the room. The only escape, except for the door, was a narrow window, which was quite a way up on the wall. The Queen's voice was saying something else outside and Meghan could hear some giggling. Surely, before too long, the Queen would enter and face her directly. This was the very last thing she needed after yesterday's nightmare.

With swift movements Meghan grabbed the wooden chair that was standing close by, placed it underneath the window, opened the window, stood on the chair and, one boot halfway onto her foot and the other boot in her hand, started to crawl out through the window. She was only a small final push from freedom when her sock slipped and the chair fell aside, making a terrible noise. Her body was now trembling with horror and Meghan tried to accelerate her escape, but she only managed to get stuck in the window. Unable to push or to pull, she was trapped, her head looking out of the window, her behind up in the air and her legs pointing back into the boot room, wriggling crazily and without control.

The Queen decisively opened the door and bumped into the scene. What an intensely uncomfortable moment this was for Meghan.

The Queen immediately called for help. She and the butler were both forced to pull Meghan's feet and grabbed her behind, so stuck was she in the small window.

After the rescue, Meghan was paralysed with embarrassment. The only thought crossing her haunted mind was that somehow she had to persuade the Queen to keep this incident secret. She pleaded for the Queen to make some excuse to everyone, including Harry, for her intended sudden departure, as she could not bear to face another day after so much struggling.

The Queen finally gave in. In deep concern, she watched after the Bentley as the butler drove out of the courtyard, taking Meghan home.

The Queen turned around, considering her excuse as to why Meghan was absent. Chuckling to herself, she closed the door behind her, ready to walk her dogs. In all her life she had always managed to get out of the most impossible situations; she surely would manage this case without batting an eyelash. Cheerfully, she greeted her corgis, which dashed at great speed towards her, looking forward to the morning stroll.

The butler had been quick to find a pair of wellies that suited Meghan. There she sat in the Queen's Bentley, exhausted but relieved that she could at least spend a quiet day without having to worry about every step she took.

She needed a break, but she knew she would return soon, stronger than ever ...

TO BE CONTINUED ...